About the Author

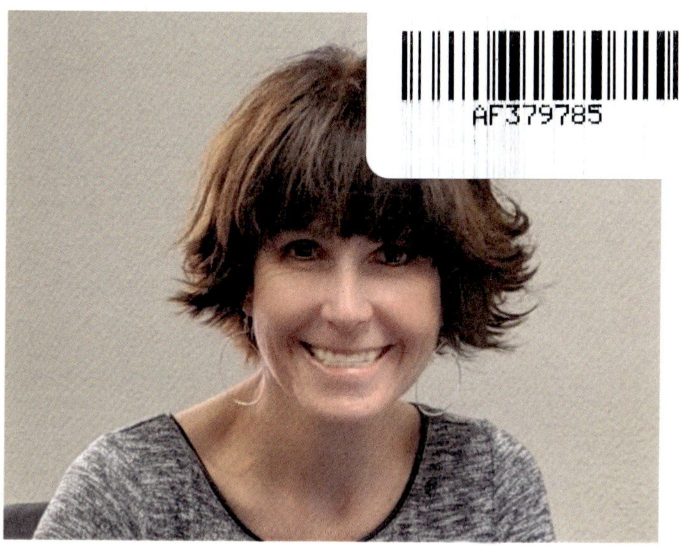

As an experienced director of assisted living communities spanning over two decades, Lillibet has a passion for helping those afflicted with Alzheimer's Disease as well as understanding and caring for their families. During her career, she has helped design buildings for this special population, and developed successful programs for memory-impaired individuals, as well as education programs for communities and families. Having penned several magazine articles about Alzheimer's Disease, she became an advocate for those with the disease and at one time, facilitated five support groups for families. Originally from Canada, Lillibet learned her appreciation of and the special magic of her grandparent's love.

Lillibet especially enjoys her adventures with her young grandson, spending time with family, friends and her dog, Bella. When she is not busy writing or helping families with loved ones afflicted with Alzheimer's Disease, she can be found running one of the many California trails or baking something delicious.

THE MEMORY TRAVELLERS

Lillibet Rowse

THE MEMORY TRAVELLERS

Vanguard Press

VANGUARD PAPERBACK

© Copyright 2024
Lillibet Rowse

The right of Lillibet Rowse to be identified as author of
this work has been asserted by her in accordance with the
Copyright, Designs and Patents Act 1988.

All Rights Reserved

No reproduction, copy or transmission of this publication
may be made without written permission.
No paragraph of this publication may be reproduced,
copied or transmitted save with the written permission of the
publisher, or in accordance with the provisions
of the Copyright Act 1956 (as amended).

Any person who commits any unauthorised act in relation to
this publication may be liable to criminal
prosecution and civil claims for damages.

A CIP catalogue record for this title is
available from the British Library.

ISBN 978 1 80016 642 4

This is a work of fiction. Names, characters, businesses, places, events
and incidents are either the product of the author's imagination or used in a
fictitious manner. Any resemblance to actual persons, living or dead, or actual
events is purely coincidental.

Vanguard Press is an imprint of
Pegasus Elliot Mackenzie Publishers Ltd.
www.pegasuspublishers.com

First Published in 2024

Vanguard Press
Sheraton House Castle Park
Cambridge England

Printed & Bound in Great Britain

Dedication

This book is dedicated to all the victims of Alzheimer's Disease, their families and loved ones. To my son, Jeffrey, who always encouraged me to write and gave me a journal many years ago to start. A creative genius in his own right. It is dedicated to my daughter, Julie, a lovely, creative spirit who encouraged me every step of the way. Both, my biggest cheerleaders. To my grandson, Christopher, the contemplative one. For him I write, hoping that one day he will read it, be enlightened, and be inspired to write. To create. To my son-in-law, Chris, whose love, support, and strength for his family, were instrumental in writing this book. To my sister, Nancy, for all of her wise advice and support. To my mum, dad, and brother, Steve, who have been so supportive all along the way, listening to my excerpts out loud. To all my family and dear friends, who listened to my ideas. Thank you from the bottom of my heart. Memories for my heart…

Prelude:

The year is 2042. The average life expectancy is now 128. The segregation and warehousing of seniors in Assisted Living and Memory care communities have not existed for over a decade. Most diseases have been cured: Cancers, HIV, Dementias related to physical causes, Heart Disease, Diabetes… Alzheimer's Disease, if DNA is tested early enough. Yet there are a very few with a predisposition for Alzheimer's Disease, that did not have the opportunity to implement the therapy cure. That is what this story is about. It's about them, their relationships, their memories, what matters most in life, the future of aging and time travel.

A story about the future, the cure for Alzheimer's Disease and making memories…

"We are future travelling through the present bringing the past along with us." Elizabeth's quote 3/2020.

Chapter 1: Dr. Clyde Abrainium

Dr. Clyde Abrainium sat in a chair at the back of the administrator's office. Quietly listening. He was feeling sorry for his sons as they talked. "They have lost trust in me, their own father. In my abilities. My cognitive comprehension." For Clyde it didn't really matter where he ended up living now that his sons had decided that it should not be with either of them or their families. "This 'memory care community', as it is known, is as nice a place as any," Clyde thought to himself. "After all, I am certain that I can find a way to visit my dear wife, Emily, every night".

Without introduction and before Alice could say hello, Jonathan, Clyde's older and somewhat detached, attorney son, started right in with questions. "Can our dad move in here today? "What do you need from us to make this happen?" He was here for a purpose. He wanted to get on with this process and on with his life.

Dr. Abrainium's younger son, Miles, was deep in thought, allowing his older brother to ask the tough questions. His face and body language made it obvious that he was having more difficulty emotionally coming to terms with this whole disease process than his brother,

Jonathan, was. Miles' mind wandered while Jonathan continued his questions. He vacillated between his previous solidarity with his brother and his questions about his dad staying home with family. Despite the ongoing challenges that presented daily, Miles was not convinced that his dad should live apart from his family. He certainly had his reservations and questions. "Are we really doing the right thing for Dad?" he thought to himself. He was hoping that Alice would answer his questions, relieve his guilt and that being here, at Greenbrier Gardens would give him a level of comfort. Miles and Jonathan had already decided together that Greenbrier would be the best option for their dad at this point. They made a pact together. After weeks of careful research and deliberation, it had been decided. Today was the day they would bring Dad to Greenbrier. They would meet with Alice, a world renowned expert on all things Alzheimer's Disease. This disease had basically been irradicated many years ago, in the same fashion that smallpox, polio, and cancers had been, making it extremely difficult to find someone left in this field of knowledge that could help them. Alice was their only, and last, hope to help their father. "She has an exemplarily reputation for her knowledge and expertise. Alice will understand what we are going through. She will offer some answers and comfort for our guilty grief."

For the past several years, their once very witty, and competent father had begun a gradual descent, to today, morphing into a person that they had difficulty recognizing. It had started when they lost their mother, seven years ago.

Miles also harbored doubts that anything would help their dad. He missed the pre-emptive therapy available to cure Alzheimer's Disease. He passed the screenings and didn't meet even the minimum qualifications for the therapy. Yet, it had happened. This horrible disease did one day take hold of their dad, changing their lives forever.

Alice directed her focus toward Dr. Abrainium. "Hello Dr. Abrainium. I'm Alice. How are you today? Can I get you something to drink?"

Dr. Abrainium responded by putting his hand up and shaking his head. "No. Thank you, Alice. I am fine."

"Please feel free to join in the conversation when you want to, Dr. Abrainium," Alice said before pivoting back to his sons. "Why the urgency for the quick move today?" Alice, the administrator, asked them.

Miles began, "Please understand, Alice. This is not an easy decision for us to make." Nodding toward his dad, he continued, "Our dad was a brilliant world-renowned physicist and scientist. He developed some very important scientific processes and theories. He discovered the basic process for time travel utilizing our own human emotional energy in part with AI and the Photon Energy Transfer process. Although Dad was unable to complete and prove his time travel theory due to this progressive disease process." Pausing briefly to swallow the lump in his throat, and blinking back tears, Miles continued. He spoke with pride. "He has many patents under his name, Including the one for Photon Energy Transfer that he collaborated on, with your husband, Max."

"Yes," directing her response to Dr. Abrainium. "You have many very impressive accomplishments."

Jonathan started speaking to help avoid going down an emotional path with Miles. A path that he didn't want to travel down. He felt they needed a practical solution here. "Yes. We have lost our dad. Lost him to Alzheimer's Disease. He has progressed to a point that we can no longer care for him. He is one of the few that missed out on the cure for Alzheimer's when he was younger. The MRP cure that your husband, Max developed about twelve years ago now? It was this connection however, that led us here to you, Alice, and we found your program here at Greenbrier Gardens.

We decided, together," giving his brother a quick sideways glance, "that you would be the best person to help him. That you could help us," Johnathon added.

Before Alice could get out her next question, Miles continued. "You know Alice. Is it Alice? Or should we call you Doctor? I forgot to ask. I am so sorry."

"Alice is fine. Please continue your train of thought," Alice encouraged.

"OK. Thank you. One thing that is important to note, is that our dad has hung onto a belief concerning our mother. Even in his progression of Alzheimer's Disease, he is convinced that he visits her every night. He talks about his visits with her as if she is still right here with us. His mind is sharp and focussed when he speaks of her and his visits. He is quite animated in his conversations. He brings up conversations with her that he must have had in years past, yet he makes it sound like he has just spoken to her. Our mum died over seven years ago. He doesn't seem to have ever missed her though. He has never really grieved. It was with her passing that we noticed his decline. His unrelenting crazy talk of visiting her. We felt that it was important for him to understand that she is gone now. When we attempt to gently remind him, he just smiles, telling us, quite lucidly, 'How can I miss my sweet Emily? I visit with her every night.' We cannot hold too many meaningful conversations with him anymore. One of the exceptions is certainly surrounding his nightly 'visits' with our mother."

"Yet, he continues to be very forgetful and has lost his ability to make good or safe decisions." It was Jonathan offering this information as he too was swept into the emotional conflict so consistent with families in this sad situation. "He doesn't know his way around the kitchen to get himself something to eat or drink. We must constantly watch his every move and it has become exhausting. We are afraid that he will somehow hurt himself if left alone. Alice, we understand that you have already helped other families that have missed out on the therapy cure. This is the only place left that does what you do. Your technologically and innovative programs here are world renowned. Do you think that you can also help our dad, Alice?"

Alice was disappointed that Jonathan and Miles had not included their dad in this conversation. His sons spoke about him in the third party, as if he was not there or that he could not understand their conversation. Alice had listened to Miles and Jonathan while also observing Dr. Abrainium's reaction and including him in the conversation. Alice was the last person to join this meeting in her office. She didn't know that before she entered this meeting, Dr. Abrainium had chosen to sit in the chair at the back of the room. She could see that he was absorbing the entire conversation, word for word, intently and deliberately.

"Listening to my sons, they think I am crazy. What I tell them is the truth. I do visit Emily each night. I know I need a little help occasionally, but I am still here. Still the same. They have stopped seeing me," Dr. A. thought out loud.

Miles and Jonathon turned to look at their father and said in unison, "You see what we mean."

Alice was all too familiar with circumstances just like the one being presented in her office today. So very sad, she thought. They need some education for sure.

Alice walked over to where Clyde was sitting, and crouched down in front of him, eye to eye, "Clyde. How do you feel about all this? This conversation?"

She patiently waited for a reply, giving him all her attention. "It is to be expected." He paused. "But not accepted." Clyde held Alice's gaze, sensing her understanding and compassion. He knew in that moment that she was someone he could trust. Alice saw something behind Clyde's eyes. Understanding. He was present. Was he holding a secret, perhaps? Alice wanted to find out more about his regular nightly visits with Emily. Alice wasn't convinced that his visits were all 'crazy talk', as his sons alluded. She certainly wanted to have a conversation with her husband, Max when she returned home. She couldn't stop thinking about what she had learned from Max about time travel. Clyde was quite lucid at this moment, but Alice knew that could also change in another moment.

Alice smiled back at Clyde and stretched out her hand, "Would you like to come for a walk with me Clyde?" Clyde took Alice's hand as he stood up. At eighty-seven years old, he was very physically fit.

As Alice and Clyde were walking out through the tall, black glass doors, Alice turned to Miles and Jonathon, who were now standing.

"We will be back shortly. We can talk more about your commitment and involvement in our program then."

Dr. Abrainium's sons looked at each other, a little bewildered, as they watched their dad and Alice exit.

Chapter 2: Alice's Husband

The Process: Capturing significant memories of people's lives, in real time, using Artificial Intelligence implants. The MRP, Memory Retrieval/Remapping Process chip.

Alice's husband, Max, had spent almost his entire career of thirty years exhaustively researching his theory to use a synthetic process to remap one's memories, creating a healthy path for new memories to travel upon. A neurologist, surgeon, physicist and A.I. scientist, Max certainly had the right combination of education and skills to ultimately realize his goal. The theory behind his process, begins with creating a new memory map to reroute memories as they happen. Next, capturing those memories as they happened, pushing them along the newly created memory path; Before diseases such as Alzheimer's Disease had the opportunity to destroy one's new memories. In order to facilitate this, Max successfully created a tiny chip device, mimicking the Hippocampus. This was perfected after almost eleven years of trial and error. The tiny chip was surgically inserted into the affected person's brain, capturing all their memories as they happened and built upon one's total memory storage.

The person had the ability to retrieve and replay those memories as any other person could, with normal brain function and without the use of this chip. Taking those memories, creating a new map for them to travel upon, store them and consciously retrieve them later, proved to be a much more daunting process. It was a process though, that Max was determined to achieve. Max shuddered to think of what could have happened, with the other, now very obsolete 'brain chip' developed and failed over twenty years ago now. Max remembered studying the failed process and theory. An Artificial Intelligence chip was inserted into the brain of a pig, which was guided by a robot and gave very basic and rudimentary directions to its brain. This was so very creepy to even the most open-minded scientists and theorists, it was doomed to fail as soon as it was introduced. And fail it did. The process seemed unethical on its face and for this reason, unacceptable to the public. However, it opened the idea of integrating A.I. with humans, to the general population. Understanding this, the world scientific community converged shortly thereafter, agreeing to put a stop to this process immediately. Max was especially happy about this outcome, as he saw only evil and destruction as the probable outcomes using this technology. No one ever wanted their brain or that of a loved one to be controlled by a robot, or an AI system to allow them to perform simple functions. This would have been no help or progress whatsoever in the continued efforts to cure Alzheimer's Disease. It would have left the AD victim a 'zombie'. Only controlling basic bodily functions. For what good purpose? The person was still 'lost.' It was something that no one wanted.

If this had been realized, what next? Could people in power introduce this to the public thereby controlling people? That was so diabolical. Max was so thankful that this was never the case. His direction, work and process were now used for good purposes. Max's process for a cure for folks with a predisposition for Alzheimer's Disease would have their memories stay intact. They would stay in control of their minds and functions. The new memory path would essentially reroute their older memories and continue to capture the new memories, moving them along the synthesized route, not allowing the disease process to destroy them. The caveat to Max's MRP chip though was that it did have to be implanted into a healthy brain. It needed to start working at capturing memories while the brain was still able to process memories normally. In this way, Alzheimer's Disease was unable to survive.

Max was always confident that he could one day achieve this process. Finally, the day had come, in October of 2036. Max had accomplished the achievement of a lifetime. He had successfully created a memory map process on which memories would travel. Together with his MRP, his hope was that no one would ever suffer with Alzheimer's Disease again. He remembered that day so vividly. It was a great feeling of satisfaction and unapparelled pride. He could only compare his feelings that day to the day he married Alice and the to the births of his two children.

Alice was right by his side all the way. She was his biggest fan and his partner throughout the entire process. He was so elated to think of all the people that he could finally help. His personal reason for pursuing this process was always foremost in his thoughts and heavy on his heart. Max knew all too well the tumultuous heartache of slowly losing someone to Alzheimer's Disease. His thoughts turned to his own mum, a beautiful, compassionate soul. A pediatric nurse who later studied and became a heart surgeon was his hero, and inspiration. She had perfected a process to help repair the hearts of children born with Atrial Septal defects. Her passion for what she did as well as her compassion for these tiny little victims and their families greatly inspired him to pursue his passion for helping others. She was also a wonderful mother, always had just the right answers and encouragement. They remained close as Max went on to study medicine and physics. He remembered her as being strong, resilient, and brilliant. Max had a very difficult time accepting her diagnosis of early onset Alzheimer's Disease. It was an eighteen-year journey that he was completely unprepared for. His father did his very best to care for her, but he eventually sought the help of a long-term placement community for her final years. That fateful last day that he had met his dad to visit his mum was stuck in his memory and in his heart. "I was able to say goodbye to her, but in reality, she had been gone for a long time before that day." Max remembered.

"Hello Dad. How is Mum today?" Max asked as he walked up to the front entrance of the memory retreat community.

"She is having a very difficult time breathing, son. The nurse has told me that it won't be long now. I came out to look for you." He paused. "I believe that she is waiting to see you today," he said with tears in his eyes.

Max gave his dad a long, warm embrace before taking his arm, the two of them walking in silence down the corridor to his mum's room. His once vibrant, witty, and feisty mum now lay fragile and weak, in the small hospital bed before him. Seeing her struggle to take each breath was almost too heartbreaking for him to endure. None the less, Max managed to lean over and give his mother a kiss on the cheek. "Mum. It is so good to see you today. "I love you very much." Tears trickled down his cheeks. He did not try to stop them.

His dad had taken a seat on the little stool next to the head of her bed and was gently stroking her hair. "You look beautiful, Tilly. I love you to the moon and back," his dad said as he attempted smiling at her. He thought he saw his mum smile back at his dad before taking what was to be her last breath.

Max stood speechless as he stared at his mum in disbelief. His tears turned from trickles to streams. Attempting to choke them back, "Yes. She is at peace now," he thought.

His dad was standing next her, holding her hand, tears also streaming down his cheeks. "Tilly, I love you. Please don't leave me yet. What will I be without you? I love you." As he watched his parents say goodbye to each other that day, his heart full of grief, Max vowed that he would continue his pursuit to find a cure for this memory thief disease.

More than three years had gone by after his mum passed at the age of sixty-eight before Max was honored with the most prestigious of awards in the scientific world, The World Scientific Life Progress Achievement Award. This very distinguished award was not easily earned or achieved. As a matter of fact, only a very few people in the entire history of this award had ever received it. This award was created in 2026 and given to the scientist that developed the cure for cancer, Lucy Jane Wentworth Favell. She was entirely brilliant of course and gave her entire team most of the credit for this achievement when accepting the award. Max remembered being present at this ceremony, Alice right by his side as she always was. Lucy's words, "If not for the enduring, relentless, never-ending hours and dedication to our cause, of my entire team, this dream of the cure for cancer would not have been achieved. I humbly accept this award and share it with my entire team. To my team! This is for you and for all of humanity." What an inspiration she was. Max was encouraged and energized by what some thought would be impossible. Yet this paved the way for all of mankind to live healthier, longer lives. It also became a bit of a springboard for Max's research. It helped Max focus and catapult him to the next level of research and discovery for his MRP. It was only five years later, that Max was recognized for his great, significant scientific and humankind achievement; his MRP. Max had achieved his goal in developing a cure for Alzheimer's Disease and honored his mother in doing so. "Sixty-eight years old is too young to die from this disease and fifty is too young to be diagnosed with it. My hope is that no one else will have to live with this disease and no loved one will have to live through the 'long goodbye'," Max concluded when accepting his award.

Chapter 3 Alice's Passion

Alice's passion for her life's work and calling of almost thirty years ago now, shows in all that she does. As a Gerontologist, Physician, Aging Researcher and former licensed community administrator, Alice was dedicated to helping the victims struggling with diseases plaguing the aging, as well as their families. Alice was particularly focussed on helping victims of Alzheimer's Disease and their families, throughout most of her career. She could not imagine herself doing anything else. However, once the cure for Alzheimer's Disease was discovered by her husband, Max, the need for specialized care communities, such as memory care, became obsolete. They shut their doors. Assisted Living communities had not existed in over a decade due to the many cures for most diseases such as cancers, heart disease, HIV. People were living long, healthy and productive lives well into their 120s, 130s and beyond. With these significant advances, the entire shift in how the aging process was managed also advanced. Care for people with any health issue, took place in one's home. With the assistance of AI and hologram infused physicians and surgeons, the need for long term care of any type became unnecessary. Minor surgeries and procedures also took place in one's home using this same technology. Homes adapted and were either built or renovated with a wellness room. Accident emergencies used drop-in pop ups and were easily facilitated at the scene of an accident, negating the need for transport to an actual facility or emergency center. This advance offered far better results in saving lives, manpower and time. In-home accidents could also typically be accommodated in the home with the assistance of AI and hologram infused physicians. This left the hospitals to efficiently accommodate major surgeries, transfer and true emergencies.

These technological advances as well as cure advances, saw a huge shift in how Alice's career changed direction too. Alice focussed her efforts on research and helping the population age better. Education and working closely with her husband, Max, took up most of her time and energy. Alice was elated and relieved at the prospect of and ultimate cure for Alzheimer's Disease. Yet, as she had devoted so much of her life to its cause, and helping others, she couldn't help but feel a huge void in her life because of it. Alice had garnered a world renowned reputation for the development of her creative and successful care therapies for the victims of Alzheimer's Disease. Alice started a program to teach families how to care for their loved ones at home. She opened a family-oriented training community where families came to live and learn about the disease process, how to care for their loved one, and then return home to live together. This program was highly successful, due to the wonderful education that Alice offered as well as all the advancements in technology to assist families once back at home. AI technological advancements had greatly impacted the ability for these folks to remain living at home with their family. Alice customized each program depending on the individual and their circumstance. Human-like robots, once thought creepy to most, even ten years ago, were now commonplace in every household. Alice employed the brightest AI engineers to customize sophisticated programs for each robot to help these victims and their families. A volunteer adoption program for those that had no family was carefully implemented. The victims of Alzheimer's Disease deserved no less. They were all very special human beings. Yes. This was a dream come true for Alice; to fulfill her true calling in this way. She had helped so many victims, so many families. "Of course, meeting and marrying Max was also part of my destiny," Alice thought to herself. "I cannot imagine what my world would be like without him. He has helped me work myself out of a job." She smiled at that thought. "His successful MRP therapy has virtually wiped-out Alzheimer's Disease for everyone, world-wide."

That was until Alice began receiving calls from all over the world. It had been over twelve years now that Max has discovered his MRP process therapy. There were seventeen people that had already begun the Alzheimer's Disease brain deterioration process when the MRP therapy was approved and began to be implemented. It was too late in the disease process to help them. Their brains were not healthy enough for the MRP therapy cure to be effective. These Alzheimer's Disease victims had missed being eligible for the cure. None of them showed a propensity for the disease or had early warning signs. Now they all desperately needed help. Alice's help. Alice was ready.

Alice was completely optimistic that Max would develop a new process that would help her residents though. "He is so close to making that happen."

Driving down the long laneway leading out of Greenbrier Gardens, that evening, Alice reflected on her day and her good fortune. She could not have imagined a more perfect setting to help AD victims than Greenbrier Gardens. The fifty-acre property, complete with horse stables, trails, a pool, tennis courts, eight separate small cottages, and walking trails were very generously donated by wealthy philanthropist, Macy Mullins. Macy's husband had sadly succumbed to Alzheimer's Disease many years ago, before Max's therapy cure discovery. Macy wanted to do everything that she could to help other families in the same situation. To that end, she decided to leave the property in a trust to Alice, that included a very large multi-million-dollar endowment to operate the property and to provide all needed care. Macy was indebted to Alice for helping her through the Alzheimer's Disease with her husband, Richard. She could not have thought of a better use of her considerable wealth than for Alice's work, much to the chagrin of her family members. Alice remembered Richard's journey and helping Macy struggle through those final weeks of his life so many years ago now. That long ago night, Alice was sitting in Macy's family room enjoying the beautiful English garden view. Macy's final words were surprisingly unexpected, yet so hopeful and very gracious. "You really helped me through my time with Richard. I truly don't know what I would have done without you Alice. You were here for me, guiding me through each step along the way. You offered me support and were always here to listen. It is for this reason that I am leaving you, my estate. Greenbrier Gardens is for you to continue your life's calling, Alice," Macy offered.

"I am completely speechless, Macy. And so humbly honoured." Tears formed in Alice's eyes that ran down her face as she looked at her hostess in disbelief.

Macy wanted to get her message out while she still had the energy to do so. Frail and bundled up in blankets, in her corner easy chair, she continued, "Further, I am also leaving a very large endowment to continue operations and provide care. I don't think that you will ever have to worry about ever running out of money. This way, families will never have to pay for the care of their loved ones. Money will never be an objection to provide the best care journey possible while they live here. I want Max to continue his research and for you to use all the advancements and technology available to help these people." With a serious and steely fixed gaze, "I know you will, Alice. It gives me great comfort and satisfaction, my dear."

There wasn't a day that had passed since then that Alice didn't think of Macy and her astounding generosity. Some days she could hardly believe it. "My residents and families have hope now, thanks to you, dear Macy." Alice said out loud to herself. "And hope is what we all need each day."

Chapter 4: "The Meeting"

Max prided himself in his ability to solve complex scientific problems. At the young age of eight, Max had already mastered a comprehensive understanding of many of the scientific complex theories and processes. He had won awards in his teen years for the development of his own processes, theories, and inventions. Now, as a neurologist, surgeon, holding PhDs in both artificial intelligence and physics, he was very grateful that he had the sense to gain the right combination of education to help him achieve his goals. He had developed the therapy cure for Alzheimer's Disease. After many years of watching his wife, Alice, help victims and families struggle with the disease and its emotional toll, Max was beyond excited to help these people. While Max's peers of researchers directed their efforts in seeking the cure for Alzheimer's Disease through their clinical trials of medications, Max persevered instead on a different, lonely path to find the cure for Alzheimer's disease through Artificial Intelligence. Max sought to develop a process that captured one's memories and generate a synthetic healthy brain map over which they could travel. Max stayed true to himself and his course, while his peers remained quite sceptical over the years. His hard work and determination finally did come to fruition. His dear wife, Alice, was right by his side all the way. She was his biggest fan. His partner. His best friend. Without her support to cheer him on, listen to his ideas and theories, he may have never achieved his goal. When Max felt discouraged, Alice was right there with words of encouragement. She reminded him why he was doing this, "Do it for your mom's sake, Max and all those sweet souls just like her. Think of all the people you will help. Will save. You are truly a brilliant hero my dear Max."

"Alice is a strong and dedicated partner." Max pivoted from the problem before him in his home laboratory to thoughts of his wife. He contemplated their lives together. Max remembered the first day he literally bumped into her. Alice was a junior and Max was a senior at Vernon High. Alice was a new student that year at Vernon. Max remembered that first day and smiled. She was running very late for her next class that first day. With her eyes straight ahead, she was intent on making her next class before the doors to her next class closed and she was shut out. She was not going to get lost another time today. She did not want to miss this class. It was her favourite subject, English Literature. With the long, seemingly endless hallway stretched before her, she picked up her pace, almost running down the hall. "I'm going to be late for another class my very first day here. I am so embarrassed. What a first impression I will make." Alice said to herself. "Maybe if I just run, I'll make it." Straight ahead and focused on the open door at the end of the hall, the warning bell had just rung. She had five minutes. She might just make it after all. Alice was so intent on her goal; she did not notice the tall young man sauntering down the hall towards her. He had his head down, buried in thought, looking down at his book. When he finally did look up it was too late. Alice had run right into him. Max's book became airborne. Alice's papers and books were tossed about everywhere all over the floor. Her glasses hurled through the air like a relentless projectile before they hit the ground and slid way down the hall floor landing just in front of her next class door. "Well, I must admit I didn't see that coming," Max said as he tried to steady his balance.

"Oh dear. I wish you would have been a little more aware of your surroundings. You didn't see me? I didn't see you at all. You came out of nowhere! And now I'm late for class!" Max countered

"No. I didn't come out of nowhere. I was walking down the hall in plain sight. And at a normal human walking pace, I might add."

"Oh no!" Alice exclaimed, not registering Max's comment. "My glasses! Where are my glasses?" Alice was frantically scrambling to pick up her books and papers all that were strewn all over the floor. Without her glasses, this was a challenging task as she could not put her notes and papers in order.

Max bent down, helping her collect her things. "Here. Let me help you." Looking into her eyes, he said, "By the way, my name is Max. Nice to meet you. And I am hoping you have another name other than 'I am late for class'."

Max's charm disarmed and calmed Alice. She blushed. "I'm Alice. Alice Cameron." Max was immediately drawn to her warm and friendly smile. He noticed her long, wavy, auburn hair and big, beautiful brown eyes. Alice took a breath and offered, "Thank you for your help really, Max. I'm certainly late for class now. I really do appreciate your stopping to assist me. I am so embarrassed as this keeps happening to me today. I have been late for just about every class. My glasses must be around here somewhere," she said, squinting, looking down the hallway. Max saw her glasses leave her face and remembered where they landed. Both Max and Alice were standing now, Alice had assembled her books and papers in her arms. They started walking toward her class door. Max stopped and picked up her wire rims and handed them to her. Placing them on her face, Alice proceeded to open the door for her class.

"I hope to see you around Alice Cameron."

Alice blushed. As she turned around, she smiled back at him. The most beautiful smile he ever remembered seeing, lit up her face. "I hope so too," Alice replied. She gave him a little wave goodbye, mouthing the words, "Thank you again."

"Yes. That first meeting was a sweet moment in time," Max reminisced. He remembered that first impression Alice had made on him. Tall, elegant and graceful. Quite pretty when flustered he noticed, during that first meeting. He remembered everything she wore that day too. A rusty orange coloured sweater over brown, blue, and tan plaid pants. A pair of plain brown flats finished off her ensemble. "It's funny how I can remember our first meeting in such detail. I fell in love with her there and then. The rest is really history as they say." Max mused to himself.

Perched atop his black faux leather swivel stool, he redirected his focus on his task at hand staring back up at him from the concrete counter, filled with beakers and microscopes. "This has got to be it. The finishing piece for the time travel process..." His thoughts were abruptly interrupted with Alice's voice. "Max! I'm home!" Alice respected her husband's time in his lab. She never wanted to disrupt his thought process. He also sometimes worked on top secret processes that even she was not privy to. Today was an exception to her rule though. She was too excited. She was sure that Max would welcome this interruption and break. "May I come in?" she asked, giving him some time. Alice was always so excited for Max to share his latest project details with her, when appropriate. "I wonder what he is up to today," she said to herself."

"Why of course! Come on in, darling." Max responded. As Alice entered his lab, it was obvious that Max was in the middle of some sort of experiment. He rose from his black swivel stool and greeted her with a kiss. "How was your day?"

"It was very interesting, Max. I have some important news to share with you." Alice needed to catch her breath and took a moment to look around at the familiar lab scene. Handwritten pages were stacked in piles in an organized fashion on Max's long stainless-steel worktable. There were various glass and stainless-steel vessels, neatly arranged on the concrete counters. The large chalkboard at the end of the stainless-steel table was filled with mathematical formulas. Max was wearing his white lab coat, with his goggles pushed back on top of his head. "It looks like you are working very hard on something very interesting. Important. Something new?" Alice asked, tilting her head.

Max smiled wide. "Yes. I will have to tell you about it. But you are first. You came bouncing in here, out of breath and in quite a hurry. It sounds like you have something important that you want to share."

"Oh. Yes. Yes. As a matter of fact, I do. Well, darling. Dr. Clyde Abrainium became my newest resident today. I know that we didn't think there were any more Alzheimer's Disease victims left out there after the sixteen souls that landed in my community and that missed your MRP cure. I thought we knew all of them. It's so very sad, Max. Dr. Abrainium, father of time travel itself. Just imagine! Could we have known? Could we have guessed that he would be a victim?" Alice paused as she gathered her thoughts. "His two sons came by with him today."

Max listened with sadness in his eyes. "Dr. Abrainium. The father of time travel. It is an honor to know him. It was a privilege to work with him on his time travel theory. As a matter of fact, this theory of his, this last piece is what I am working on right now." Max paused. "I am truly sad to hear this news. However, coincidently, I am currently working on completing what Dr. Abrainium was not able to complete. His time travel theory. The last piece: the actual travel not just the theory. I am so close. If I can get this last piece, it may very well help Dr. Abrainium and the other sixteen residents that are in your care Alice."

"What do you mean, Max? How can time travel help these people?"

"Alice, think about this. If I can solve this last piece in Dr. Abrainium's time travel process, in all practicality, time travel would be real. Be possible. I could travel back to a time when they were healthy, capture their healthy memories and use my MRP chip to help them in our time. Look. I have all his original formulas right here. I am very close. Alice, Dr. Abrainium was so close to finishing this. I have been working on this tirelessly. It is very exciting. I am convinced that time travel is indeed possible now! A specific time and date or even circumstance can be pinpointed and travelled to."

"Wow! That would be incredible Max! It gives me chills to think what this could mean for these folks. Not to mention what it could mean to the travel and tourism industry!" Alice exclaimed.

"Now Alice. Don't be cheeky. You know that this is top secret. No one can know that I am working on this and that I am so close. You know it could be very dangerous if the wrong person got a hold of this. We could never travel back in time to attempt to alter our current fate. I believe that I have worked out a way to accomplish this too. Others may want to travel back for selfish reasons with the implicit intent to change their own fate. They may not be concerned about how this may affect life and the world as we now know it."

"Max. That is such a scary thought," Alice exclaimed. "I am not convinced that he did not finish his formula and theory. That is what I am looking at today. I believe it is right here. Hidden in plain sight. I can feel it." Max added.

"Max. I believe you are right. I also believe that I may be able to offer proof. During my meeting with Dr. Abrainium and his sons today, some interesting information emerged. It seems that Dr. Abrainium may indeed time travel. He may well have finished his practical theory and decided to bury it recognizing that it would be very dangerous if the wrong people ever got a hold of it."

"Alice, how would you know that he has time travelled?"

Alice continued, "He has been telling his sons that he visits his wife every night. Emily passed away over seven years ago, yet he has never mourned her, and he certainly doesn't seem to miss her. He speaks of her in the present tense, as if he has regular daily conversations with her. His sons don't believe him and think this is just more proof that he has Alzheimer's Disease and that it is progressing. This is one of the reasons why he is my newest resident at Greenbrier. His sons are convinced that he has Alzheimer's Disease, or he is one of those cases where the genius ends up drifting off into a different world. I am not convinced that either is true so I have had all reliable tests performed and I will have my answer tomorrow morning. Max, he is so sweet, smart, and humble. I just want to help him. To think that you may have discovered a way to help him is absolutely thrilling!" Alice paused and then continued. "You know, Max, the more I think about it, the more I am convinced that the reason he has never mourned his wife is because he really does visit her every night. Just like he says. He is not hiding it. He knows that no one will believe him. That's his secret. He has kept this last piece a secret for some time." Alice looked straight at Max, with all her usual passion she said, "Max, you have been working on this time travel theory for years, searching for this last piece. I think Dr. Abrainium has it. You are probably right. This last piece is buried right in front of you, within his theory. Dr. Abrainium's visit to see me today convinces me. If anyone can find this last piece, it's you, Max. It was meant to be you."

Chapter 5: Neuman, "The Travel Thief"

A once trusted peer of Max's, and a renowned neuro-physicist in his own right, Neuman also had been working on a time travel theory. However, Neuman's work was unbeknownst to Max. It was also not disclosed to the world scientific board that helps regulate and research such work. Neuman kept his work a secret. Neuman justified this to himself, as 'everyone would just steal his ideas.' While Max worked tirelessly to uphold and follow good ethical procedures on each of his theories or processes, Neuman followed quite a different and selfish path. Neuman had always been very clever all throughout grade school, then high school and college, often working in partnership with Max. Max was always happy to have a colleague of Neuman's calibre to collaborate with. Neuman was an old and trusted friend. Or so Max believed. Max's long history with Neuman gave him no reason not to trust Neuman. Neuman had patents for a few of his earlier, simpler inventions that were truly remarkable in helping mankind and society. One that he was quite proud of was the magnetic personal vehicle travel process that he developed twelve years ago. This is the main vehicle travel process accepted and used today all over the world. His magnetic rover process replaced all older gasoline and electric powered engines. The magnetic hover process was clean, easy to use and efficient, as well as a quite inexpensive energy. Neuman received the highest, very prestigious world scientific award. He was highly honored for his invention, partnering with all major vehicle manufacturers to quickly implement this in all their vehicles. This invention revolutionized world travel at the community level. It seemed that the scientific world had moved on from Neuman's remarkable invention though. Neuman had not had a significant invention since. Nothing of any consequence. He grew frustrated that Max had been catapulted into the scientific invention world with his MRP therapy and his other discoveries. As a result, Neuman felt like he was always in Max's shadow. Second best. Max had all the awards and all the glory. Neuman was convinced that it was his turn now. He deserved recognition for his work. He deserved the highest honour award. All the accolades.

"Max will not beat me to discovering the time travel process. This will be the biggest and most significant discovery of all time. 'That was a pun'." Neuman giggled to himself at his brilliant humour before he was off again on one of his diabolical, dubious thought processes. Neuman set up his next experiment in his own home lab. "I am so close. I can travel back and use the information I learn to change my own destiny and history. That way, I will be the one who invents the MRP process and the other discoveries. I will be famous and wealthy. I will be unstoppable. I will rule the world. I may never die. I will be respected by my peers. I deserve this. I have worked so hard but somehow Max beats me to the finish line every time. Success is imminent. I can feel it."

He continued his thoughts, "I will no longer feel inferior as someone who was brought up in struggling financial circumstances, while my peers had family and financial stability throughout their lives. I never knew my dad and mum. I lost them so early in my life. I was only nine. My aunt had to raise me. I know that they would both be so very proud of me if they were here today. They could celebrate my achievements with me as I receive the highest scientific award ever, for the time travel process. Once I change all of this, they will be there to stand with me. Once I change my history."

Yes, Neuman was envious of his peers over years of observation. He was especially jealous of Max, although Max never suspected it. Max had it all. A loving, stable, devoted family. They all stuck together through thick and thin. They celebrated and supported each other. Growing up, Neuman was always remembered and invited to Max's family celebrations. This was especially true after Neuman lost his mum and dad in a tragic car accident as a young boy. After that tragic accident, the McTibbitt family always made sure to include Neuman in their own family events and celebrations. Neuman was different then, growing up. He was principled, humble, thoughtful and gracious. Pretty well adjusted. He wasn't always so resentful or vengeful...

In the tight knit, affluent suburbs of the early 90s, streets displayed cozy two storey homes with pools. Mums drove mini vans and dropped their kids off at school. Dads had the income to make it so. Neuman was grateful back then. He appreciated the lifestyle too, until the accident happened. After the memorial service, his family home was sold. He had to move to the apartments complex a few blocks away with his Aunt Lila. As a result, Neuman spent countless hours in the school library over the years, learning everything he could about the universe and how it all worked. Neuman was fascinated with this study and threw himself into learning, often coming up with his own theories on space and star travel. He was enthusiastically interested in astronomy. It was in grade seven that his teacher, Mr. Drexol, recognized Neuman's passion and future potential in the world of stars and physics. Mr. Drexol encouraged him, often giving him special projects for extra credit. Neuman excelled in this field. Mrs. Wesley, the school librarian, allowed Neuman a dedicated area at the back of the library to read, study and work on his extra projects. "I have never seen someone spend so much time in a library or be so devoted to reading every new book that comes out about astronomy," Mrs. Wesley would say to Neuman when he visited one day. "Look what came in today, Neuman. A brand-new book on galaxy interpretations. It's called 'A Trip in Star Time Through our Galaxy.' I saved it for you to read first. I will expect a report on it of course per our usual arrangement Neuman." She smiled warmly at Neuman. Mrs. Wesley enjoyed listening to Neuman's theories and discoveries about what he had learned. It gave her heart great joy to know that she was helping him learn.

Neuman stared at the new book and excitedly exclaimed, "Oh wow! Thank you, Mrs. Wesley! I will read this now."

Mrs. Wesley knew he would read that entire book today too. "You are most welcome! When do you think that you will have our galaxy all figured out Neuman?" she asked.

"Hopefully very soon., Mrs. Wesley," Neuman responded as he gathered his new addition along with his other study material and headed off to his special study space.

Neuman was quite alone in life now. But here, in this quiet space, he could dream. He could create a different world for himself. Here he travelled through space and time. All things were possible, and he could make time stand still. He imagined his life differently as he suspended time and changed it to allow for his dad, mum and sister to be with him today. To change the circumstances the day the accident happened. "They would have stayed home in the storm that day instead," he thought to himself. Sometimes, Neuman imagined himself to shed his thick black rimmed glasses and be tall, strong, and fit. Not so geeky and gangly looking.

Over the past eight years, Mrs. Wesley had watched Neuman grow and gain amazing knowledge in his chosen area of passion. "You are so brilliant. You will be a great inventor or scientist someday, Neuman. You could be the next Einstein," she observed that he was quite unique in his abilities to quickly absorb information and then regurgitate it very simply. It was her continued encouragement and interest in his wellbeing that influenced him throughout the rest of his life. Her kind and positive words stayed with him, keeping him out of trouble at times over the coming years.

Neuman remembered the one day that was a significant turning point for him. It was a usual Thursday afternoon library visit. Mrs. Wesley was especially excited to welcome him that day.

"Neuman! I could hardly wait to see you today! Look! Look what came in today!" She pointed behind him, directing his attention to the large window at the back of the library.

As Neuman turned around to look, he could hardly contain himself. He could not believe what he was looking at. It was about the most beautiful thing that he had ever laid his eyes on. "Wow! That is completely exquisite Mrs. Wesley!" Neuman declared. Can I have a closer look? Can I use it?" He was almost dancing toward it.

"Well of course you can! It just arrived this morning and it is all set up now. It is waiting for you to test it out."

"Oh boy! This is great!" Neuman exclaimed as he quickly opened the door to the other side of the large window. The room that would now forever be referred to as 'the telescope room'. He walked all around it, taking it all in with a very excited Mrs. Wesley watching the boy intently. Neuman looked over at Mrs. Wesley. "May I look through it?"

"Yes. Of course you may. I have permission to allow you to be the first to use it," she answered, delightedly.

Neuman began adjusting the telescope height and other parameters to his own. "This is the most beautiful telescope I have ever seen!" he exclaimed.

"Yes. Now you don't have to imagine anymore. You can really look at our galaxy and the stars. You can put your accumulated knowledge together in a practical way now with this very powerful telescope, Neuman." Mrs. Wesley responded.

"And expensive!" Neuman said. He paused and looked over at Mrs. Wesley. It had just occurred to him that it must have cost someone very dearly to donate this telescope. It didn't appear out of nowhere. "Where did this come from?"

"It was donated to the school from Dr. Clyde Abrainium."

"Someday I want to have enough money and influence to donate such things and have my name engraved on silver plaques to commemorate me." Neuman thought to himself. "Dr. Clyde Abrainium? I will have to look him up. I have never heard of him."

Chapter 6: Sally Fitzgerald

One of Alice's seventeen amazing residents was Colonel Sally Fitzgerald.

Colonel Fitzgerald was the first African American female Astronaut. Alice was quite impressed with the Colonel's credentials, career and her story. She remembered reading about Sally Fitzgerald's heroism years ago when the tragic incident happened on one of her missions. The year was 2029. Sally's five-woman crew were the best of the best. Sally had hand selected them specifically for their expertise on what was to be a routine mission to the moon's space station. A mission that was important as part of a three-step mission. Sally had already completed six other similar missions as well as four other much more complicated and longer ones, 332 days in space. Sally was selected for this mission because of her impeccable record as a strong, intelligent leader. Four of the five crew members on this mission had accompanied her on three prior missions and had successful experience. Sally trusted them with her life. Lynne, Nadia, Delphine, and Grace. The fifth woman crew member, Kelly, was a new astronaut and this would be her first mission. Kelly was excited for this experience. She had exceeded all the rigorous physical training requirements and was at the top her class for the written exams. Sally was confident that this routine mission would give her a solid experience and help establish her career. After all, she would be with five other very seasoned astronauts, and they had all spent months training for this mission together. Simulating the steps and roles each would play until there was perfection. They lived and breathed this mission. The day had come. The moon crew that had been living at the space station for six months were counting on them to deliver their supplies so that they could complete their twelve-month mission and return home. Food supplies, communication from family, equipment, life sustaining supplies and robots were all on board. The lift-off went smoothly, and the crew's entire voyage was captured in real time for the whole world to watch. Alice recalled being inspired as she watched these brave women leave the Earth in the fire spewing capsule. Always fascinated with space travel, she was excited to view their space walk and share the experience with Max, son, Will Henry and daughter, Adelaide.

Embarking from the space craft, Nadia led the team out. One by one they slowly bounced along, all in their state-of-the-art attire, connected by cables for safety. With the aid of Delphine, Nadia carefully opened the attached storage capsule, allowing the 'resting' robots to also embark. Max, Alice, Will Henry and Adelaide were completely mesmerized as they watched the robots assemble their supplies and transport them to the space station. Three of the robots were to stay at the space station, while the remaining three would travel back with the crew. Sally was at the back of the six-woman crew line with novice, Kelly, in front of her. As they had practised many times on Earth, they began their 'spacewalk' to the top of the space station to change the power accelerator. This was the second piece of their mission and they worked together with the technical robot. It was a marvel to watch this experience and it was completed flawlessly, as practised and without event. The technical robot installed itself into the docking station to monitor the new accelerator. The crew had begun their assent toward the space station where they were to live for two days before beginning their journey home. Sally gave the thumbs up to all her crew. She was very proud of how well they did. Novice, Kelly, did a great job too. About halfway down, Sally noticed that Kelly was fidgeting and looked like she was in distress. Kelly was pulling at her helmet and turned toward Sally frantically now, pointing at her face. Sally gave directions to her crew to stay in place, allowing Sally to get close to Kelly and access the issue. To Sally's horror, Kelly's helmet's face shield had a crack in it. Kelly was struggling to breath, and it was apparent to Sally that Kelly may not make it back to the space station. They each had more than enough oxygen to make the trip back, but Kelly's oxygen was leaking right out of Kelly's damaged helmet. Sally stayed calm and directed her medic, Lynne, to quickly open the first aid kit and use anything she had in it to stick on the leak. "It's OK, Kelly. Lynne is going to repair your helmet so that you can breathe better. It is good that you are remaining calm. I am going to turn the oxygen flow valve down a little lower to help."

Lynne grabbed the adhesive tape from the kit, placing it on the crack. Kelly began calmly breathing again. Relieved, Sally knew they had no time to spare if they were to get Kelly safely back to the space station. She gave the command to continue. They continued their journey to the space station. Sally was relieved when she saw the end in sight. So far so good. Kelly began grabbing onto her helmet again. Sally instructed the crew to unhook the cable between the front three crew members and Kelly. Sally would stay with Kelly and assist her. Reluctantly her crew followed her instructions. Sally reached Kelly to find her breathing labored. "Don't give up Kelly! We are so close! Come on we can make it if I must carry you back," Sally implored Kelly. Kelly was giving up. Kelly had a look of despair and loss of hope in her eyes. Sally had never experienced this before in any of her crew members. They all went through vigorous training together to avoid these circumstances. Some called it 'space crazy'. Kelly was immobilized by panic and fear, losing precious time, minute by minute, to get back to safety and more oxygen. Sally took a hold of Kelly and secured her cable directly to hers, carrying her back to the space station. Sally stayed calm and confident. The Space Station medics immediately took Kelly to the space station's hospital to get her the much-needed oxygen and to stabilize her. They worked hard, doing what they were trained to do for several minutes before determining it was too late. They had lost Kelly. Colonel Fitzgerald was beside herself with grief. She reviewed the entire voyage and the events that led up to this point over and over in her mind. She could not think of anything she would have or could have done differently. Before the mission began, the space team as well as Sally herself, had checked the equipment and more than protocol determined. Kelly was well trained, at the top of her class, never showing signs of psychological weakness. that this was ever possible. And yet it was human nature to be unpredictable at times. The equipment should not have failed. Kelly should not have failed. There was a thorough investigation into the equipment failure, as well as an exhaustive look at Kelly's background and training. Sally was absolved of any wrongdoing. Sally blamed herself for all the failures of this mission. Sally could never forgive herself.

"Yes. Such a tragic event for dear Sally and her otherwise impeccable and remarkable career. It's very difficult for her family to see her now, who she has become. Sally does not even know her daughters anymore. It's crushing and so sad to see her decline and her daughters' despair."

Sally was brilliant and contributed substantially to the space mission. I wonder though, if Sally were to travel back in time, would she do anything differently?" Alice asked herself.

Chapter 7: Mum's Tea

Having tea with her mum was one of Alice's most favourite small pleasures in life. It was a welcome family ritual passed on through her family generations. Growing up, when something was troubling her, Mum instinctively knew that a hot cup of tea and the ensuing conversation would help make troubles melt away. Any school day or relationship problems would all be solved during these tea-time conversations. Things would be put into proper perspective. Whether Alice received a 95% on her school project when she expected a 100% mark or she had a crush on a boy at school that didn't seem to even notice her, Alice would leave the teatime table with a feeling of calm and resolution, if not a renewed sense of purpose. "Mum was always able to put a fresh face on any problem that came my way," Alice mused. Most of the time though, teatime was a welcome time to talk, share dreams and hopes for the future, reminisce about a funny show they had watched together or connect. A simple delightful tradition.

Once Alice had her own home and family, Alice's nanna came by to visit for teatime too. Nanna would comment during these visits, "Alice, you are the only one in the family that knows how to make a proper good cup of tea." Alice remembered thinking that this was a high compliment indeed. The family after all, had many other members of aunts, uncles and cousins. Alice recognized that these traditions were an essential foundation to connecting with family. They made for great memories too. Alice carried on this teatime tradition with her family. Many conversations resulted in problems being sorted out. Sometimes tears dared to attempt to interrupt, but resolutions were determined, with smiles and laughter replacing those tears when all was said and done. The love, care and joy she held for her family was carried over to her extended family of the residents that she cared for. Her biggest joy was to spend time with her family, her children, grandchildren, Mum, Dad, aunts, uncles, cousins, siblings. Her husband, Max. Daughter, Abigail, son, Tom Henry and her precious grandchildren. Her family. her home. Alice's refuge. Each day spent with her residents, though very joyous and unpredictable, she was very happy to come home to those who meant the very most to her. Each night upon entering her front door, she was reminded of how very important her family was to her. She never took for granted, the memories that she cherished. Her comfortable home that she shared with Max. Every day Alice made a point of committing her life to memory. She never wanted to forget the sound of Max's voice when she arrived home. "Welcome home to the now my Ally Queen!" Max greeted her. Or how tragic not to remember the sweet innocence of questions from her grandchildren

"What's that for, Nanna?" her seven-year-old grandson, Jack Oliver, would ask.

"That is a grasshopper, Jack Oliver."

"Oh, I know that it is a grasshopper, Nana. But what is its purpose?" Sometimes nannas had difficult questions and make into simple answers. These are the components of life that helped shaped Alice's career choice, her dedication and compassion for her residents.

Chapter 8: The Drive Home

Driving home as so many times in the past years, Alice took those thirty minutes or so to unwind and recap the day in her mind. It was easy to do in her new Magnetic Hover Rover or the Mag Rov as the folks shortened the name to. Organizing her thoughts and significant events of the day, one by one she reviewed each of her seventeen residents placing any of their issues in order in order of importance in her mind. She reviewed the activities of the day. Lavender Flowers played the piano for us today. Fun and lively. Most of the residents joined in. Singing, laughing, clapping their hands. Sister Harriet O'Connor even got up and danced. Smiling and keeping time with the music, her long gray ponytail swinging back and forth. Hands in the air, she motioned to Jason to join her. Noel sat in his chair smiling, continuing to tap his feet and clap, although a little offbeat. Nurse Ben, Activities Director, Greta and Executive Chef, Shane joined in the fun. Mel, Eileen and Cash, all nurse companions staff, were singing, dancing while encouraging those that were able to get up and move. While others stay seated, staff danced with them while in their chairs.

"Wow! Harriet! You really have some rhythm!" Ben exclaimed. Harriet felt so free and so strong. It was easy to see how she loved the piano music by the way she was moving. The happy smiles on her face. She seemed like she was suddenly transported to a different world. Another time. Two other residents, Brad and Dana were singing loudly, though not always entirely in key, remembering all the words to that good oldie 'Brown Eyed Girl' by Van Morrison. Music Director, Lavender Flowers, continued playing the piano, perfectly flowing into 'Can't Stop Dancing' next and his group of resident fans were right with him, singing, clapping, swaying, tapping their feet. Nancy and Milly were on their feet moving around the floor, dancing like no one was watching, effortlessly flowing across the expansive hardwood floor surface of the activity centre. Employees, Greta, Shane, and Cash became the resident dancing partners. Cash really had some great rhythm keeping the beat. He was so much fun to watch his interaction with the residents. His energy with them was contagious and so wonderful to see. Clearly his energy was a positive influence as evidenced by the residents' faces. What a joy to behold. This moment in time. This moment of the day. Our own little happy world. Welcome to a moment of happy. Music was truly the common denominator for all to unite and to enjoy. To be completely alive. To ignite memories. Memories of the dance, memories of the words that they remembered. Alice was at once completely enchanted in and in awe, heartened by what she was witnessing here on this day. The music therapy program was certainly something that she could be very proud of. She and her staff had accomplished great things with this program these past few years here at Greenbrier Gardens. Music is timeless. Memory invoking. Alice and her staff had created their own world around the music for her residents. Alice is education and music therapy boy her own personal theory that she had developed early in her career. It was also a powerful part of the education she implemented with the residents' families.

She taught them music therapy, the power of music and how to use it instead of other therapies. Today was certainly a great example of how well it worked. The power of music therapy created a healthy environment with fewer incidents or falls or other related typical health issues that occurred in this type of disease process. Music gave her residents energy, or peace and tranquility depending on the situation and something to look forward to. Alice learned long ago that dance was about the best exercise therapy you could have. It used memory: the dance steps, it involved others: the social part we all need, and the music itself and the way it makes us feel. Music gave them balance. Yes. This indeed was the common denominator. With just the right song, it could carry you back away in time back to a place in your memory. Doctor Abrainium was no stranger to this fact either. He had discovered this missing piece for his time travel theory years ago. Music, he discovered, was a big piece of his time travel process theory.

Chapter 9: The Day

"How was your day?" Max queried Alice.

"My day was filled with fun and discovery," Alice answered. "I have a new resident and his family that have begun the program today. He has moved all his belongings in already. A Doctor Clyde Abrainium. Do you remember him? Didn't he discover a time travel theory?" Alice asked Max.

"Yes, Doctor Abrainium. Brilliant. I studied under him I studied his work. His theory of time travel was plausible. He could never prove that it was possible though. He inspired me to continue my work on my MRP. I owe him gratitude for this. Without his inspiration and the basic concept of his theory I don't know if I would have been able to finish my theory and then prove it. I have not heard anything about Doctor Abrainium in over ten years. Tell me how it is he came to be at Greenbrier Gardens, Alice?"

"He came to visit me today with his two sons. They were both very distraught and felt that they had nowhere to turn. He certainly met the legal and medical criteria to reside at Greenbrier Gardens and complete our program. Dr. A is beyond our program in many respects though. He knows something. There's something in his eyes. A secret.

I can see it. His sons do not seem to be aware. They assume that his talk of time travel is part of a cognitive disability and pure confusion. They shared that he believes he visits his wife at night. And they don't believe him. I believe that's his secret. I will be helping the staff tomorrow night so I will have an opportunity to observe him. I am just so curious about his life in about what the son said about him. Max smiled at his wife of thirty-five years. He adored her. The passion she had for her calling never ceased to amaze him. Her compassion unyielding. Max moved toward Alice, gave her a loving embrace, bending down to gently kiss her…

The doorbell rang. "Oh, that must be Adelaide!" Alice said. "She's dropping off Jack Oliver and Jane Lily for the weekend." Curious, contemplative, and full of questions, seven-year-old Jack Oliver is Grandfather Max's constant companion while he visits. Max loves his questions in his pure uncomplicated way. It gave him pause to consider things differently. It put things into a certain open perspective. To three-year-old Jane Lily, Jack was her hero. For Alice there was no greater joy than to spend time with her grandchildren. "Mom! Dad! We're here!" Adelaide yelled in.

Chapter 10: The Adjustment

Doctor Abrainium was getting adjusted to his new environment at Greenbrier Gardens. Alone for the first time in a long time, he surveyed his surroundings. Quietly. Taking it all in. Happy that it was his own familiar furniture and belongings that appeared in front of him. The quilt that was a wedding gift to he and Emily over fifty-three years ago now. Somewhat tattered but very neatly folded at the end of his bed. Yes, his bed. The same bed that he and Emily had shared for their entire marriage. Handcrafted of solid mahogany wood. It had stood the test of time. His matching dresser end tables comforting indeed. Copies of his degrees and his awards, his patents all hung with care and arranged in a collage on the longest wall of his new one-bedroom abode. Spacious enough Clyde thought to himself. And so familiar. His mind traveled back to Emily and her thoughts when she first saw the furniture, "Wow that furniture is just beautiful," exclaimed Emily. Emily loved the beauty of natural materials. The fact that Clyde's brother and father had lovingly fashioned these pieces in their workshop just impressed Emily even more. "I never ever want to give these pieces up these are beautiful and they're so precious that your dad and brother made them just for us. Life just doesn't get any better," she smiled and laughed. "Come here, Clyde. I think we should try this out." Emily was pointing to the bed and tapping her hand on the mattress.

Emily was beautiful, tender hearted and beguiling. Clyde remembered that night particularly. The first night in their new home after their ten-day honeymoon. Of course, Clyde was all too willing to accommodate his young wife. Clyde reminisced about those early days. Mostly so happy. And sometimes awkward. His memories flooded his mind as often they did. No sequence of date or time they just presented themselves in no order. Like a book collection sporadically tumbling from the shelves. And onto the floor. Upon picking them up, one by one, not recognizing the content of them at times. Not knowing what shelf to be placed back upon. In his mind frantically attempting to pick up each memory and put them back in its rightful file. To be retrieved later at his beckoning. To make sense of it when he called upon it. His memories were becoming more and more disarrayed. Indeed, tumbling out of his mind with the files all jumbled up. No organization. No sequence. Clyde was still cognitive enough to realize that it was becoming more difficult to recognize his memories as they came to him. Part of this horrible disease process he said to himself. Instinctively Clyde walked over to the bed fixated on the left side bedpost he reached for it. Forcefully he turned it to the left before turning it to the right. Twisting it off at the top Clyde peered down inside. The shallow hollowed out cavity held a secret. Known only to he and Emily. Reaching down with his right-hand Clyde retrieved the small, polished mahogany wooden box. Sitting on the side of his bed Clyde closed his eyes. Smiling he took a deep breath and then sighed. Holding the little wooden box ever so tightly he drew it toward his heart. He could still remember this as if it was yesterday. The first time this box was used. Clyde's disciplined regimented and organized approach to life was wonderfully balanced by his wife Emily's carefree happy relaxed style. There was one time though that this wasn't so. This balance wasn't there. The day Emily had been working all day on a special project on a special art project for her students while in her back studio. Her students at Lady Back elementary where Emily taught music and art. Emily woke up that morning feeling so very inspired. She had been thinking of a new way to help, inspire and develop her student's appreciation for the arts. This would be great she thought springing out of bed. It was 5:00 AM. Emily went for a thirty-minute power walk in the neighborhood to polar thoughts together she could hardly contain her excitement. This is it. Her mind was racing. Getting this project together and presenting it to the board. Surely this would allow them to realize the value and importance of this program to continue it on. She had a quick shower. Clyde was awake. Giving him a gentle kiss, "I made coffee and juice for you darling downstairs. I hope you don't mind missing me at breakfast today, but I have the most inspiration ever for my project. I need to begin it right away."

Clyde remembered the conversation and smiled. "Of course, you can't waste your inspirational ideas!" he said. "You need to pounce on it right now." He blew her a kiss as she breezed out of the bedroom door. Clyde jumped to his feet and reminded her, "Don't forget our faculty dinner tonight darling. At the Smythe Lindens?"

"Oh, I will be ready!" she shouted back happily, while bouncing down the stairs and out the back door.

That Saturday, Clyde spent most of his day at his research lab working tirelessly on his time travel theory. His work was so important to this possibility. He had published a paper on his theory. His peers reviewed it and even though they mostly considered it fantasy-like and highly improbable they could not dispute the facts that he presented. It was brilliant. At thirty-seven years old he had worked on this for over a thirteen-year period now he was being presented with an award for his theory as well as a promotion at the college. He was excited and so looking forward to the night. With Emily by his side, he felt like he could do anything. It was getting late he thought to himself I better lock things up here and head home to get Emily. He was so eager in anticipation yet also somewhat nervous for the future of that evening. Arriving home and turning the key in the front door he said, "Hello darling I'm home right on time as promised." Entering the front foyer and discovering it to be lightless Clyde became a little concerned. Racing upstairs Clyde called out Emily. Arriving on the top of the stairs Clyde was greeted with the same silent, lightless hallway and bedroom. No sign of

Emily. Almost 5:00 PM Oh dear he thought to himself I do hope she's ready. Surely, she realized how very important tonight is to me. She must be in the studio, Clyde thought to himself. He rushed down the stairs through the kitchen and out the back door. Down the garden stones to her stereo studio. Looking through the studio window there she was. What a sight to behold. Paint everywhere. Even in her hair. Headphones on. Grinning ear to ear. Swaying to the music. Clyde entered her sanctuary swiftly. Looking her straight in the eye, "Emily what on earth are you doing?" he questioned loudly.

Emily pulled her headphones off. Her astonished deer in the headlight look gave him his answer. Yet Emily also felt compelled to say out loud, "Oh my goodness! I lost all track of time! why it's after five o'clock!" Emily could see the bewildered disappointing look in Clyde's eyes.

She walked over to him to give him a hug and a kiss, but Clyde was angry inside and managed only "Please Emily. Go get ready. You have only fifteen minutes or so to do so." In all that time of seventeen years that she had known Clyde she had never felt his anger towards her. Yes, Clyde remembered that night. Emily looked gorgeous as she ascended the stairs of their home twenty-two minutes later. The navy-blue satin dress fit just right. Her beautiful long wavy auburn hair, curled and shiny, bounced around her shoulders as she floated down the stairs. On the bottom stair Clyde was ready with her jacket. Her long diamond drop earrings played peekaboo with her hair. She shot Clyde her dazzling smile. Clyde's heart melted. He could not stay angry at her. His Emily. Even if they would be a little late on this very important evening. She had his heart. She knew it but she never took advantage. Yes, the evening went as planned. It was a wonderful evening. Clyde opened his eyes and looked up at his award in the black and gold frame on his wall that he received that night. Shifting his gaze back to the little box clutched in his hand he slowly opened the lid. Inside there it was. Still the first note that Emily had left for him. Faded and yellow now and gently folded, still held together with the hair clip she wore that night. He gently removed the clip and unfolded the paper. He read her handwritten note as he did each night since. "Remember Me, the one who loves you so. More than words. More than time. It is time that pulled us apart tonight. And time that mended our hearts. Meet me in your dreams tonight for our heart time. All my love. All the time, Emily."

"Sweet Emily, I miss you so." This note began a longstanding tradition in their years of marriage. Sweet hidden love notes tucked inside the little wooden box for the other to read and to keep mending their hearts. And to travel back in time. Clyde's thoughts were quite clear at this moment sitting on the edge of his bed. Emily could not have known then. But she held the key to Clyde's time travel theory. Yes, he discovered in this moment that key. Clyde was able to unlock that final time travel piece because of her.

Chapter 11: Saturday Evening at Greenbrier Gardens

Walking down the hallway of Greenbrier gardens on that Saturday evening, Alice expected everything to be quiet and lights out. She expected that all residents would be sound asleep, peacefully, somewhere in dreamland. All except Sally. Sally was at a point in her disease journey where day and night had no real meaning. Sally could not discern between the two. Sometimes Sally was up and awake all night and asleep during the day. This seemed to be her individual time clock, despite best efforts to help her into a regular schedule. Alice and her staff of course went with Sally's schedule. Alice had peeked into the Theatre room to see Sally when she first arrived, she was sitting there happily in one of the comfortable recliners cozily wrapped up in a blanket with fluffy pink slippers. Her assigned caregiver, Laura was sitting next to her. They were both laughing at the old movie that was playing on the big screen in front of them. "I just love to see that." Alice quietly said to herself. "Hopefully this movie will help Sally fall asleep." As Alice's experience was that she often did. "Sleep is so important to my resident's health and well-being." Helping them fall asleep naturally with a regular schedule was the goal. Sleeping medications or other such aids, was not Alice's preference. Physicians and families certainly agreed and appreciated this too. Quietly closing the Theatre room door behind her, undetected, she said to herself "my sleep is important too." Visiting her residents that night, she wanted to make sure that all was calm and quiet in the community. Continuing her evening walk down the apartment corridor area, Alice stopped at each apartment and ever so quietly peeped in to check to find each resident soundly sleeping in their beds. Nurses, Mary and Sam, continued to do their rounds, on each corridor, alertly listening, watching, logging into each resident's robot communication system. They were constantly looking for any unusual activity with the residents left in their charge. They were ready to respond if any unusual activity with a resident was detected. Two additional nurses, Amy and Rose, were also doing rotations, walking the halls, checking on the residents and monitoring the robot systems. IT specialist, Sean, was monitoring the entire system in the IT room. Alice felt truly blessed to have such a wonderful, caring, dependable and attentive staff. The nurses were specifically trained for these roles and truly dedicated to the care of their residents. The building was especially designed to give each resident their own individual experience. Privacy and space were important elements in the design process. Each resident's personal life profile was studied to include their preferences when creating each living space. experience and environment and monitoring while allowing complete visibility in vantage point from either end of each hall. This gave families and staff Peace of mind when their loved ones or loved ones were here and they weren't here for the program. Having five great care nurses, nurse aides, janitors, security chefs, at night as well as the robot monitoring system certainly gave Alice a special piece of mind. Wristwatch sensors monitored residents' vitals and movements within their homes while robots monitored the environment all sending signals back to the nurses in the station. However, even with the well-trained staff in place in all the technology available at her disposal, Alice visited Greenbrier Gardens often and often at night randomly at different hours to check on things. Doctor Abrainium had been a resident here less than forty-eight hours. Alice was especially interested to see how he was settling in during the nighttime hours. Yes. Allison could run a report at home and get his vitals and see everything that was going on from her home office but there was nothing like good old fashioned human contact she thought. I enjoy visiting at nighttime to visit my staff. Alice never visited empty handed. Food was the gift of choice for her staff. And tonight, was no different when she brought in specially baked items and coffee drinks for her staff. She approached Clyde's Garden condo door #29. Alice was surprised to see Waldo the robot positioned on watch outside of his door. Waldo's sole purpose was to be present inside the apartment to monitor the environment. Oh, my, Alice exclaimed. "Waldo. What on earth are you doing outside of doctor Abrainium's apartment." All robots were programmed in designed to the specific resident needs inside their apartment. They were connected to the programs inside the apartment and responded to the environment of the resident in their needs they could think for themselves to a large degree but could not respond to the resident's request when it was inherently unsafe to do so this was not consistent with their programming. There was something alarming to see Waldo outside of Clyde's apartment.

Waldo responded to Alice. "Man hunting for lightning bugs position on this side of the door is best place to find lightning bugs I was told."

"Waldo. You need to be on the inside of the door in your docking station. Helping doctor Clyde stay safe."

Waldo said doctor is safe. All vital stable, sleeping. Why would Clyde do this Alice was stunned. How was Clyde able to manage this. "How long have you been out here?" Alice asked Waldo.

"Forty-three minutes." Waldo said he just inside the one-hour time for nurse rounds thought Alice. Waldo unlocked door #29.

Alice knocked and called out as robot unlocked the door. "Doctor Abrainium? This is Alice. May I come in?" Alice did not wish to interrupt Clyde's sleep, but she was concerned and wanted to make sure he was indeed sleeping. After about a minute went by and no answer. Stepping inside the dark apartment Alice heard voices. Quietly she stood there listening outside his bedroom door. She gently knocked on the now open door. "Doctor

Abrainium? Are you OK?" Still no response. Alice softly opened the door and peered into the room.

Adjusting her eyes to the darkness, she heard a hushed woman's voice whisper, "Goodnight my darling. Remember Me. Remember time." "Goodnight darling." Clyde's voice in a hushed response. Alice's eye adjusted as she stepped in further. She peered towards Clyde's bed and was quite surprised to see Clyde sleeping peacefully. Alice turned her attention to the patio. The door was closed tight. The kitchen was clean and tidy. The living area too. Clyde's entire apartment was void of any visitors or disruptions. Bewildered, Alice stepped back toward the entrance way. She needed to gather her thoughts, and quietly closed the door behind her. She leaned backwards on the door for reassurance and gazed over at Waldo. "Waldo. Do you know anything about what happened in Clyde's apartment tonight? Did Clyde have any visitors, Waldo?" Alice knew there was just no way anyone could penetrate the perimeter of the gated secured building. There were nine check points of close security and identity. "Whomever Clyde was speaking to tonight, must have come in with someone today. I will need to check the security footage and virtual visitor log." Alice decided. "This will be a good place to start my investigation. Either that or someone is playing a very unkind trick on me." "Waldo, I do not know how you got yourself outside of Clyde's apartment as I know that I instructed you to stay inside of his apartment. Please go back inside to your station and do not leave his apartment tonight unless instructed by me."

"Yes ma'am. I will go in now and stay inside Clyde's apartment. I will keep Clyde safe. Instructions from Alice only. Not Dr. Clyde." Waldo repeated.

Alice's racing heart was beginning to slow down and feel a little more normal. If Waldo had been in the apartment this entire time, Alice would have been able to retrieve a report of this entire episode and she would have her answers. Now, it remained a complete mystery. Part of the mystery included how Waldo ended up outside of Clyde's apartment. He was programmed to respond to only her or one of the three nurses on duty tonight. Confident that Waldo was inside Clyde's apartment now, keeping him safe she quickly down the hallway towards Sean and the IT office

Chapter 12: Max and His Grandchildren

Max was always quite happy to spend time with his two grandchildren. Especially now that they were old enough to ask interesting questions. The macaroni and cheese dinner was two hours in the past now. Baths were done, pajamas on. Max sighed to himself. Alice made sure that all tasks were completed before she left the house to visit Greenbrier Gardens. What are you working on now Grandpa?" serious in his seven-year-old voice, Jack Oliver asked? Partly because he knew it was now his bedtime, he was trying to stretch out the time he could stay up. Also, because Jack was particularly interested about what his grandfather did in his lab. He wanted to understand how things worked and why. Jack wanted to be part of solving all these science's biggest mysteries with his grandfather. He was sure that he could really help his grandfather to this end.

With Jane now in his arms, ready for bed, Max looked down at young Jack. Big blue eyes, so innocent inquisitive staring back at him. Max ascended the stairs., speaking to Jack. "I am writing a theory to use my MRP together with time travel, Jack. I want to capture memories of the past. I am quite close actually and very excited."

Now Jane's interest was piqued too. Especially upon hearing the time travel words. Jane's favorite television program was 'Time Dragons.' An action-packed animation where the heroes traveled back in time to help people in the present time. "Oh!" Jane excitedly exclaimed. "Can we see it?"

Max did want to share, and safely, his theory so far with his grandchildren. Alice would not be home for some time, so he thought about it. "No harm in taking a few minutes to help them understand what I'm doing", he thought to himself. A big grin stretched across Max's face with the thought of the children's excited expectations and interest. "All right then. Let's go have a look at what Grampa has so far. But we need to get straight to bed afterwards, right?"

"Right," Jane chimed in.

Still carrying Jane when they arrived at the entrance door to his lab, Max gently put her down to free his hands to unlock the door. Max and Alice's house was somewhat older and was built way back in the 1950s. It was solid. They had made many modern technological updates to the home. A modern-day ranch complete with The Secret Garden out back. A state-of-the-art laboratory was built as an addition shortly after he and Alice bought the home such a long time ago now. Solid concrete floors and walls with thirteen-foot ceilings were the foundation of Max's laboratory. Although there were no windows, there were four skylights and what Jane referred to as a magic back door. Magic because it was inconspicuously located at the back. It only appeared like magic when Grampa pushed all the right buttons. Lining up his right eye to the camera on the door leading into his lab then placing his palm on the entry panel Max said out loud "Open sesame." The door responded by clicking and Alice's voice announced. "Access granted, 30 seconds." Next, Max turned both the top and middle handles to enter. Jack and Jane were wide eyed in anticipation, patiently holding their breath. Each time they were able to join their grandfather in his lab was so exciting! They knew the rules. They could come in, sit on the comfortable stools Grandpa had provided just for them and wait for further instruction. The children were old enough now to understand they had to stay still and quiet while visiting the lab. They knew they could not run around or touch anything in Grandpa's lab until Grandpa gave them special permission and instruction. Once inside, Max helped Jane and then Jack to sit on the stools. Stainless steel refrigerators, large refrigerator freezer, and a double burner cook top lined one wall. A computer with concrete counters on the other side. One counter held beakers, tubes, interesting vessels, magnets, and electric wires. The large eight-foot counter in the middle displayed the most updated computer system complete with AI integration. Max had built this himself and continued to update as needed.

"Oh, Grandpa where is it?" asked Jack. Hardly able to contain his excitement. "I want to see some magic Grandpa!" exclaimed Jane.

Max patiently responded, "Oh you see, Jane, Grampa has to set a few things up here first." He told the children.

Max then commanded the AI: "Irene. Start then MRP time travel." Eyes wide, sitting three feet away, Jack and Jane were riveted on the scene in front of them as an image of a young woman appeared. However, Jack was not to be fooled. He recognized this person. "Why that is just a hologram of Nana!" Jack exclaimed. Somewhat perplexed. He had seen this already before. "Just like those ancient Star Wars movies!" Jack exclaimed. Jane was still impressed though, as she did recognize her Nana at twenty-two. "It is magic Grandpa." "Well. It's not exactly a hologram Jack. This image or time spirit was captured in the year 2012 when your Nana was just twenty-two years old. It was part of an experiment I was working on back then." Max began explaining. "I have not been able to complete my theory of time travel back to a specific time. However, I've been somewhat successful in sending back a sort of synthetic person. A hologram prototype and then bringing a specific time spirit forward to our time. This proves that time travel is possible. I am so close for a human to travel back to a specific time that I choose. I want to try that next. It is complicated though, kids. There seems to be a time vortex that gets in the way at times and makes the travel unpredictable. I am missing a piece to this puzzle to resolve this issue." "What is a vortex, Grandpa?" asked Jane.

"Good question Jane. A vortex is like a hole or a gap if you understand."

"Like a bubble?" Jane asked.

"Yes. Like a big bubble Jane. That is a very good description, Jane." It suddenly dawned on Max that this was a very good probability. It was more like a bubble than a hole. It was a void that was encapsulated. "I will remember that." Max thought to himself.

"Oh grandpa! I understand," Jack interjected matter of factly. "Then you must either smash that bubble to pass through or become part of the bubble to continue traveling. Isn't that right Grandpa?"

"That's exactly right Jack." As max adjusted his math calculations to confirm. "You are on the right track. I am attempting to travel back, and this vortex is prohibiting my smooth travel process. There seems to be no way around or through it at this point. Your idea of smashing it or traveling inside this vortex bubble may be the answer to my dilemma. Instead of me traveling back in time, when I test my theory, pieces of time are floating forward. Pieces of memories." By talking this through and having the opportunity to explain this part of his theory to his grandchildren, max was able to identify another possible theory. Max's ideas suddenly solidified and came to life as part of the most important puzzle pieces came together. Max knew that if he could somehow travel back in time to help capture these important memories, he could use his MRP to retrieve and help these last few victims of Alzheimer's disease that were now analysis program and care. Max was excited and had a renewed energy to move forward and test this new theory. "You know what you two?" Max asked Jack Oliver and Jane Lily. "You both are so very amazing and precious children. You have the best ideas and questions. Is it OK for grandpa to use your ideas and work on with them for this experiment?"

"Yes grandpa. Jane shouted.

"Of course, Grandpa." Jack was serious and contemplative. "Please show me as soon as you have it. We want to see it in action."

"Show me magic," Jane excitedly added again.

"Yes. I certainly will at that time. Magic show is over now for tonight though. It's bedtime. Magic dreams await upstairs in your bedrooms." Max said.

Max left the lab with the children in tow and exactly as it was. No one else was home, so he wasn't too worried that anyone else would go in and mess things up. He helped Jane and Jack up the stairs to their bedroom and tucked them both in. They were quite exhausted, and Max watched them as they said their goodnights and drifted off to sleep. Max returned to his lab to return things back to their positions, turn out the lights and secure the door behind him.

Chapter 13: Neuman's Mistake

Neuman knew Max was working on his time travel theory. He also knew that Max was close to having it become a reality. Neuman kept a close watch on Max's comings and goings. Looking through the back skylight to Max's lab Neuman could not see everything that just happened before him, before Max turned out the lights in his lab. However, he was hoping that his X1Z image duplicator would have captured what his eyes did not see. Much more vivid in detail than an ordinary camera or old iPhone his ex IZID offered an exact replica of the events in detail almost like it was better than being right there. Neuman was excited to get back to his own home studio and lab to review the details that had just been detailed before him. He knew he could beat Max to the final discovery of actual time travel and become famous. Ultimately the wealthiest person in the history of the world. More than that, time travel, thought Neuman, would make him immortal. This was the ticket to live forever and to control everything. I am the one who has been working on this theory and formula for such a long time after all, I helped Max in college with this. I should be the one to finish it. Control it. Patent it as my discovery. Neuman was essentially a good person not so long ago. Neuman grew resentful over the years though ultimately becoming obsessed with this one discovery as he knew it was significant. He never to be doubted or looked down upon again he deserved to complete this period to take all the credit for this discovery. Neuman had become dangerous in his obsession. No one was really paying much attention to this though. And Neuman was glad about that. What Neuman did not know yet though, was that Doctor Clyde Abrainium had already discovered his own time travel process. He practiced time travel in secret. In secret that was, until Alice had happened upon him and had witnessed it tonight.

Chapter 14: Alice's Discovery

Placing her palm on the security imprint shield on the door it allowed her access, Alice Mctibbits access granted. Alice looked up to see all twenty-seven screens on in real-time monitoring each robot of each of the resident's condo homes. She quickly glanced around for Sean one of her night shift AI engineers. Not seeing him at first, she darted around the IT office and found Sean on the floor. Sean was starting to sit up feeling groggy and rubbing his face with both hands. Sean looking up at Alice. "I am so happy to see you. I am not sure what just happened or how long I've been on the floor. I was in the monitor chair checking all systems at 6:51 PM. That's the last thing I remember."

Alice was speechless. She was relieved that Sean was OK but needed immediate answers. Her resident's well-being in safety or always for number one priority. "It's a good thing that I have AI in place to monitor the humans and humans in place to monitor the AI," Alice thought to herself. "Are you OK Sean?"

Getting to his feet Sean responded. "Yes, I believe so." Sean responded.

"OK. I am glad to hear that," Alice quipped. "Please take a seat right here in this chair," pointing to the swivel chair in front of the monitors. "I'm calling Ben in to help."

Ben, a senior nurse practitioner, arrived within minutes. "Hi. I am responding to your alert request for assistance." Ben said as he entered the IT office.

"Sean had a bit of an episode tonight, Ben. He had a period tonight that he doesn't remember what happened.

Ben began taking Sean's vital signs, blood pressure, heart rate and checking his eyes. "His vital signs all seem normal." Ben offered. "How are you feeling now?" he asked Sean.

"I feel fine." Sean answered. I will run some rests, finish the incident report with test results and send it to the system for you to review Alice." Ben said as he left.

"What happened just before 6:41 PM, Sean? Do you recall anything?" Alice asked.

"Yes. I certainly do," Sean answered.

Alice explained some of the strange happenings of the evening to Sean. "Sean this night has been so completely unusual. Particularly involving our new resident, Doctor Abrainium." Alice said. Alice looked directly into Sean's eyes and thought that she noticed a bit of avoidance and fear in his eyes.

"More unusual than what you came upon tonight with me? What exactly do you mean by unusual?" Sean questioned.

Alice took a moment before responding, carefully. "I mean it can't be a mere coincidence to what I just witnessed and finding you here on the floor. Upon checking on all residents tonight, I came across Waldo outside of Doctor Abrainium's home. Perplexed by this of course, I questioned Waldo. He responded to me that he was directed to station himself outside of Clyde's door #29 to catch fireflies!"

"Why that's absolutely bizarre!" Sean responded. "The robots are programmed to follow our specific voice commands only. They are programmed to respond to the resident needs through the assessment of the environment only. Otherwise, we would have a serious problem on our hands. Especially knowing how sadly confused some of our residents are. It's a real mystery, Sean. Perhaps Clyde himself was able to override the programming? He certainly has the background for such things. He is cognitively aware most of the time." Alice was sure to emphasize the word 'most'. "Even if he was able to reprogram the robot, why would he do that? What is he trying to hide from us? What happened tonight in his apartment that he didn't want his robot to capture and be aware of?"

Sean paused before asking her, "What do you think happened, Alice? Looking at the common area monitors, Sean began assessing, trying to glean any unusual movements outside of Dr. A's apartment. Alice was intently reviewing the monitors with Sean as he moved through the sequences. A completely synced report generated, documenting the events captured. There were no cameras installed inside resident homes, due to dignity and privacy issues. The individual robots stationed in resident rooms were installed to monitor only recording air temperatures, air movement, energy, doors opening, faucets, fridge closing, windows open, steps on the floor, body temperature, hunger and thirst levels, anxiety levels etc. All in place with appropriate consent of course. No recordings of any type were allowed though. Sean said, "Upon review, from 1:00 PM, when I started my shift to the present time of 7:36 PM, everything looks normal."

"Yes. I'm looking at the same thing you are Sean and I also see that. The report also indicates that Waldo was stationed in his number 29 docking station with no movement." Sean has this ever happened before. Can you please troubleshoot and run another back report? How could Waldo follow Doctor Abrainium's direction? I need answers to these questions right away. I need to understand if this is a technical or human error."

Sean immediately began a new data search while Alice watched on. "There must be a technical malfunction of some kind, for Waldo to respond to Doctor Abrainium. I will need to bring Waldo in to do a data program search on him. There is still nothing showing up here." Sean offered.

Alice added "I keep thinking that Doctor A. may have somehow reprogrammed Waldo. What do you think Sean? Is this a real possibility? Is this the only explanation for Waldo to be reprogrammed?"

Sean said, "Yes. It seems quite plausible for someone to do that. But it would need to be intimately familiar with this technology to understand how to reprogram Waldo. Either that or another fluke malfunction that was missed. Doctor A would have to override the program himself but that would be so highly unlikely. How could that be even possible with his Alzheimer's Disease? It would take such focus and concentration for an extended period." Sean asked.

"Well, Doctor A is a world-renowned Noble Peace Award recipient, Highest of Honours, Science Award recipient, physicist and scientist. Absolutely brilliant. You are right though, Sean. He would have to plan it and have clarity for an indefinite period to complete the task. He certainly has the knowledge and skill set. It is the time part that I am having a difficult time understanding. Perhaps he did it in stages. He does have his moments of clarity." Alice stopped short of adding more of what she witnessed and more of her theory for it. "It is best to keep that information to myself," she thought. Alice could not explain hearing a woman's voice in Dr. A.'s apartment tonight. Alice heard a woman's voice coming from his bedroom area when I went to his apartment to check on him. Dr. A. granted me permission to enter, I opened the door, looked around to find Dr. A. in his bedroom his bedroom and see who it might be in his bed falling asleep. It was indeed strange to find him almost asleep and no one else about at all. I have an inclination that the incident has something to do with Doctor A.'s time travel and the secret he seems to hold. Alice hesitated again to say more as she stood there engrossed in her thoughts. She had sudden feeling of foreboding and heeded her gut instinct before saying more. Instead, Alice heard herself telling Sean, "All our residents are safely nestled in for the night Sean. Can you please replace Waldo with another unit immediately and work on Waldo tonight for me?"

"Yes of course Alice." Sean responded respectively, showing signs of relief that Alice was exiting. "Everyone will be fine tonight. I will make sure of it. I can handle things as usual with the other competent staff that we have here. You should go home in confidence and enjoy your grandchildren's visit."

Alice wasn't quite sure if it was the tone of Sean's voice or the way he was so dismissive with Waldo or both that had Alice questioning Sean's behavior. "This episode tonight, isn't consistent with his usual behavior," Alice thought to herself. All of Alice's staff were completely vetted, had superior training, knowledge and experience. Sean was especially strong in his chosen field of all things IT and AI. He was personally referred to Alice from one of her trusted school friends for his remarkable skills. However, the fact that Sean was Neuman's nephew had Alice take extra measures for the vetting process. Sean was a tall slim guy who preferred to wear the black rim glasses instead of having his vision surgically corrected. He was almost the spitting image of his uncle, Max's nemesis, his Uncle Neuman. However, Sean at just twenty-six years old, was honest and dedicated to his work. Another brilliant young man, Sean was passionate about using his talents and gifts to help others. This was not lost on Alice and was obvious from the start. Alice felt very fortunate and blessed to have Sean added to her strong and dedicated team. Sean replaced Waldo with another robot, Eli, before Alice began her trip home and began the process of deprogramming Waldo or so Alice assumed…

On her way home from Greenbrier, Alice certainly had more questions than answers.

Chapter 15: Jack Oliver and Jane Lilly

Jane Lily and Jack Oliver were sleeping soundly. Max was relieved for this and somewhat proud of himself that he had managed this task. Max ascended the stairs and remembering to go back to the lab to make sure everything was put back in place. Upon reaching the lab door, he thought he heard some scuffling noises on the roof. A squirrel? At the same moment Alice's magrov pulled into their garage. Max heard the door close. The side door to the house opened. "Max!" Alice yelled in. Her voice was earnest. "I have something I need to discuss with you."

Max turned to respond to Alice, leaving the lab door partially open and unsecured. "Welcome back home. You have been gone a little longer than usual tonight darling. I received your text about wanting to share something important with me. What is it, Alice?" Max asked.

Alice reached up to give Max a sweet 'great to see you again' kiss on the lips. Taking a moment to pause and admire her husband strikingly handsome face, she preceded to say, "We should talk in your lab where it's private. I was just on my way back in there to do a little cleanup. I had Jack and Jane with me earlier tonight to show them what I've been working on."

Alice was quite aware and involved with all of Max's theories and experiments. Especially this one. His time travel theory. "After what I witnessed tonight, I believe that what you've been working on with the time travel is the same thing that my dear Doctor Abrainium has already figured out." Now both were inside Max's lab. The children's monitors were on. Alice felt comfortable to explain what she had seen and heard in Doctor A's condo home this evening. She wanted to let Max know about Waldo and Sean and her feelings about Sean.

Max listened intently to Alice's story and what happened that evening. Max was quite familiar with Doctor Albanian's discoveries. more specifically with this time travel theory. Max was curious to understand what had transpired with Doctor A tonight. While listening to Alice's experience, he was excited to think that Jack and Jane given him perhaps the last part of his theory to put into practice. "It sounds like Doctor A has really been able to travel. We can't be so sure, but it does sound like Doctor A was able to time travel. I do have some questions though that can only be answered by Doctor Clyde himself. Let's say we head into Greenbrier Gardens tomorrow morning after breakfast. You know how Jack and Jane loved to visit the residents there.

"Especially during horse therapy time," Alice added. "I had planned to bring you all along with me tomorrow anyway so Jack and Jane could enjoy the horses."

Taking Alice by both hands and drawing her close to him he gazed down at her, "Has anyone ever told you that you are the most beautiful and brilliant compassionate administrator that ever walked the earth?"

Alice melted into her husband's arms. She truly loved Max and felt so very blessed that Max obviously felt the same way about her.

She smiled up at him and replied, "Only my husband says that to me."

"Well, your husband is an astute judge of character."

Locking the lab door behind them Alice and Max climbed the stairs to head to bed for their much-needed rest

Chapter 16: The X1ZID

Back in his studio, Neuman began the process of deconstructing what his X1Z ID had recorded expertly and patiently allowed the images to come to life before him. Max's process, step by step, Alice's image, the intimate conversation with his grandchildren Jack and Jane Lily. Their important revelation questions, Neuman ran through the process three times before he noticed the missing piece. Eureka. Neuman exclaimed to himself. That's it. His heart skipped a beat. I can now go back. Travel back in time to before that fateful accident with my parents. I can change it. Make my whole life better, period, and in the process claim the victory for this process.

Neuman could be famous and rich he began to put together and finish the missing pieces to this theory showing that it's practical to time travel and before anyone else gets to it. I need to speak to Sean he thought to himself. Sean can assist me with this and be the necessary time monitor to make certain that I get back to this time safely. Sean can provide extra information that I need regarding Doctor Abrainium. Neuman worked diligently until the wee hours of the morning until his theory was complete. Excited and relieved to have made this accomplishment even if I did need to use the work and divine coincidence of Max's work, after all I've been working on this longer than Max. I deserve this more. Max is already set. He developed the MRP. He is world renowned already for his development he has received many awards. It made him infamous for all time. It made him a wealthy man too. Neuman mused, he should share the spotlight. I mean no harm I just want what is due to me. Neuman thoughts were moving in a direction to justify his motives. His actions. It's not stealing. It's completing what I started so many years ago I can recreate this. My life will be the way it should have always been and soon. Neuman was so sure that this was his that his fear was buried.

Chapter 17: Greenbrier's Horses

"Nana! Nana!" Jane Lilly's sweet, excited squeals arrived in Max and Alice's bedroom only seconds before her small bare feet could be heard.

Alice opened her eyes to meet Jane Lilly's big gray eyes peering out from under her bangs, inches away from her own eyes. Jane earnestly patted Alice on her hand and then on the shoulder. "Nana, you have to see come and see!"

Max was now quite awake. It was 6:00 o'clock AM after all. The time that most three-year-olds began their day. Max laughed, "Well, Nana, you had better go and see what it is. OK Jane. Let Nana get her housecoat and slippers. Hurry Nana!"

As quickly as she could, Alice jumped out of bed putting on her slippers and grabbed her housecoat. Jane grabbed her nana's hand to pull her out of the bedroom door and across the hall to the children's bedroom where Jack was anxiously awaiting their arrival.

"Is Grandpa coming too?" asked Jack.

"Look, Nana." Jane pulled Nana to the window to see what Jack and Jane were so excited to share.

"Wow. That is totally marvelous!" Alice exclaimed.

"Yes, it certainly is." Max was standing over Alice's shoulder by now. "That may be the best and most colourful touchable rainbow that I have ever seen, Jane."

"It is spectacular!" said Jack. The vivid and colourful rainbow truly lit up the entire sky. It glowed, stretching right across their English garden. The end of it landing just on the other side of Alice's studio. It looked so tangible and touchable.

"Can we go outside and touch it, Grandpa?" asked Jane.

"You can't really touch rainbows Jane. You can only look at them. They are a reflection from the sun after a rainstorm," he added, "like Grandpa's holograms. Just like the one we saw last night of Nana. It's there. It's real. But you can't really touch it."

Jane Lilly still seemed somewhat perplexed. Alice chimed in. "There are many things in life that are real, Jane. Like Nana's love for you and Jack. You know it's real, don't you?" Jane Lilly nodded her head yes, while looking up at her grandmother. "It is real, but you cannot touch it. You experience my love in the things that I do for you and say to you. That is how you know that my love for you is real. Our experience with the rainbow is to see it. That is how we know that the rainbow is real."

Jane repeated, "Experience. Ok, Nana."

Alice turned to meet Max's eyes. "I do believe that explaining things to a three-year-old is much more difficult than explaining your theories to your colleagues, Max."

"Yes. I quite agree with you Alice," Max responded before continuing with his hologram explanation to Jack. "As I said, Jack, rainbows are somewhat like a hologram and that you can see them, but you can't touch them. However, one main difference is that holograms are man-made images and we control them. Rainbows just show up unexpectedly, like an endless surprise. When all elements are just right, they gloriously show themselves. As if to say, follow me and I will show you the way to the other side of the sky. Without warning or announcement, they show up. Then they disappear just as quickly. That is where the similarity ends though Jack. It is a beautiful rainbow, Jane."

Alice looked down at her granddaughter lovingly who was so completely fascinated with this rainbow. The children were quiet, looking out the window. Alice changed the subject, "Let's all get dressed and have breakfast, shall we?"

"OK Grandpa!" Jack's voice trailed as he dashed into the bathroom and closed the door behind him.

Alice looked at Max, "I'll help Jane get ready and meet you downstairs for breakfast in a few minutes," she added, "we are all taking a trip to Greenbrier this morning Jane. You can ride your pony."

"Oh boy! My pony!" Jane squealed.

It was almost 9:00 AM when Nana, Grandpa, Jack Oliver, and Jane Lilly arrived at Greenbrier Gardens. The rainbow stayed vivid, to Jane and Jack's delight, followed them all the way there.

Chapter 18: The Laneway to Greenbrier Gardens

Driving up the long, winding laneway to Greenbrier Gardens always brought Alice peace. She felt grounded. She sometimes had to pinch herself that all of this was real. During her many years of administrator tenure, she never experienced this feeling when working for someone else or for a large corporation. Alice remembers when assisted living was a thriving industry it was all but obsolete now. Greenbrier Gardens was the last community helping elderly people and to include Alice's 'family involvement program' that she was aware of. Alice remembers long ago when she was an administrator asking herself that question what a true Alzheimer's care environment would be like if money was not involved. If there were no profit. No one to benefit financially. Just build a community specifically for these residents. Have the best care the best programs the best environment all the best therapies food sleep everything that we have here. And to educate train and involve the families immerse them in the care for their loved ones. Yes, she was astounded that day back in March so many years ago now when she was handed this property in central Ontario, Canada. As if the deed wasn't surprising enough a very large endowment was set aside in a trust managed by Alice that would cover all expenses for these people for a very long time. The property taxes, the staff, the programs, the food, the materials supply, absolutely everything with all taken care of. All were considered when Macy set this up.

Macy had lost her husband to Alzheimer's disease several years ago. She stayed on the property until she herself passed away some years ago. She left her entire estate including 12.8 billion dollars that she knew could never be spent in her lifetime. Her husband, Richard Belfry, was a pharmacist and investor. Richard was a kind and generous man who was always assisting those who could not afford their expensive medications back then. Before medications became mainstream and affordable for all. He would be an astute student of technology companies and discoveries based on his hunches he invested in a stem cell research company whose stocks went through the roof in a short period of time. With that, Albert continued to invest, amassing great wealth that he used to help others who eventually succumbed to Alzheimer's Disease. Although his initial stem cell research investment company had developed a process to help heal a reverse some of man's most dreadful physical diseases it did not come up with a path to cure help with people with Alzheimer's Disease. Alice knew she was completely blessed to be the recipient of this truly magnificent property and having the money to offer the ultimate program. These last handful of people with Alzheimer's Disease or her precious charge on a journey with Alice as the ship's captain. Their well-being and safety were her biggest concern always. Laughter, having fun. Alice wrote the script for this Alzheimer's disease community setting years ago before she ever knew she would have this opportunity. As if in a dream yet it had miraculously become a reality for her. Yes, Alice wanted to pinch herself this is exactly what any person suffering from Alzheimer's disease needs and deserves.

Chapter 19: A Beautiful Summer Morning

It was a beautiful end of the summer morning. Not too hot. Not too cold. The sun was shining brightly. Wonderful gentle breezes floated through the open windows. Greenbrier Gardens was certainly displaying all its summer splendor. Tall mature trees. Maple trees and pine trees draped the laneway which was lined with wildflowers and tall grass. Lush lawns sprawling across the property. The horses were relaxing in the shade in their pasture. "Oh, look! There's Dodi! My pony!" squealed Jane. She could hardly contain her excitement.

"Yes, Jane," Alice confirmed. "There is your pony, Dodi. Let's wait to stop the Magrov before we get out." Alice looked to the back seat lovingly smiling at her granddaughter. Making sure she was still all buckled in.

"You're really a good driver, Grandpa." Jack said.

"Well, Magroves nowadays aren't so much something that I need to drive, Jack, or navigate. However, you know when I was your age, believe it or not, we had something called cars. They were powered by gasoline. They had four round rubber things called wheels or tires that touched the ground as we drove along the road. We had to be able to steer and navigate."

"You mean cars did not have a magnetic force to navigate Grandpa?

"We didn't have magnetic lanes."

"They touched the ground Grandpa?" Jack questioned.

"Yes Jack. Just like those old photos I showed you. Remember when we visited the museum last year? There were cars there too."

"What a funny name, 'cars." Jack offered.

"Yes. Cars had to be manually driven. They had some programming technology, but not anything like what we have today with our Magroves. Magroves are programmed and you don't have to drive them. They drive you."

"I didn't know they really existed. Even though I have seen them in the transportation museum. It is still hard for me to imagine, Grandpa." Jack said, "You couldn't program them either? Is that right Grandpa?" asked Jack. Although he already knew the answer.

"That's right, Jack. Things have evolved and now this is so easy to drive."

"When can I sit in that seat, Grandpa? I already know how to program the destinations. I showed you that I can already." Jack anxiously queried.

"You will still need to wait a few more years, Jack. You need to be sixteen years old. You need some experience and be able to discern possible danger changes, redirect the vehicle if needed. These are sometimes quick decisions that come with life experience. Don't be too anxious to grow up Jack. It will be here before you know it." Grandpa assured him. "Enjoy being seven years old. You are making memories today to keep forever and to share someday with your own grandchildren, Jack. It's okay to take your time and enjoy the learning process."

"I don't know how not driving is helping me stay and enjoy being seven, Grandpa. I already know how to do it. That's not going to change now." Jack attempted his best rebuttal to his grandfather's sage advice.

Max was always surprised by his grandson's challenges to his own philosophies. Although he probably shouldn't be. He learned a lot from Jack too. More than Jack even realized. Young minds aren't encumbered or cluttered. Max secretly wished that he could somehow harness that young mind and innocence into another process and have it available to all humankind. "If everyone could keep and maintain that child inquisitiveness and innocence the world would be a better place for sure. Our minds would be open. Free to roam and discover. Not already fooled into thinking that they had all the answers as most adult brains really don't. Be open minded. Like my darling grandson Jack. Like pretty much any seven-year-old." Max mused. Their Magnetic Rove was approaching the end of the long winding laneway and Max brought it to a stop. In a stop hover position, the seatbelts automatically unbuckled, and the two front doors opened. The side steps presented themselves so that Max and Alice could exit. Next, they assisted Jack and Jane safely out of the vehicle. The excitement of the children was obvious. They both love to run and play here there was so much land and so many things to discover. Every time they visited, there was still something new. They also loved to visit the people who were lucky enough to live here in a place like this. Jane Lily always commented on how she wanted to live there. The open minds and loving hearts of the children had a remarkable and positive effect on the residents here. The children benefited too of course. They made special enduring relationships without prejudice or boundaries. There was no fear in getting to know these residents. They were not afraid of older folks with cognitive disabilities. Not knowing how to behave when around that was not even in their thought process or vocabulary.

Jack Oliver knew each of the seventeen Greenbrier residents by name. Jane Lily almost too, but she certainly remembered their faces and smiles. "Let's go visit with miss Sally, Joe, and Edger! See how everyone is this morning shall we? We can all ride together to visit the ponies and horses." Jack said.

"Oh, Nana, yes!" Jane agreed.

Jack was at the front door waiting for his nana. She is the only one of their group with the right biometrics to open the front door. Once inside, happy, upbeat music could be heard travelling down the hall to their ears. It made Jane Lily dance her way down the hall. Swaying back and forth, she led the way with Nana behind her. Approaching the large, open entertainment area of the community, the music became louder and the song lyrics clear. The residents were all singing the chorus together of that old song. "You're My Brown Eyed Girl." Alice thought 'this can't get any better." All the residents were present and engaged in the music. Rare indeed that all would be together and completely in sync to the music and beat.' thought Alice. Staff members Veena, Jake, Fred, Mona, Frank, all happily singing along with the residents. Frank was playing the piano. Alice noted that Doctor Abrainium was not there though. "Perhaps he is sleeping in on his first morning. Or having a quiet breakfast." Alice recognized that although socialization was a very important component to her program, and greatly encouraged, each resident settles into their new home differently. The upbeat music took its effect on Jack and Jane too. They were enjoying the music, smiling, spinning in circles while clapping their hands to the beat.

Resident, Sally let out a little excited scream when she saw Jack, moving toward her, she bent down to give him a kiss on the top of his head. Indeed, the resident demeanors were happier overall when the children were present. Alice stood next to her husband placing one hand on his arm and the other on the right side of her mouth, she whispered, so only he could hear. "Doctor Abrainium is not here. Yet everyone else is. I need to go and find out why. I'll be right back if you can just stay here and keep an eye on Jack and Jane."

Max nodded his head. "Yes. Of course."

Alice was already hurrying down the corridor to Clyde's apartment home. Clyde came across as quiet and reclusive. A very private individual. Not someone to be too social. Alice could respect that as she considered herself to be of the same kindred spirit. It was Alice's job to offer social engagement to her residents that they would particularly enjoy and be involved in. Music was the common denominator to keep residents socially connected and involved. That is why they all were there this morning. So true for Dr. Clyde? It was not unusual for her residents to be engaged in various activities throughout the community and throughout the day pursuing their interests or abilities. It was also not unusual for residents to take a nap or choose to eat a meal in their apartment home. However, it was certainly unusual for all residents to enjoy the same activity at the same engagement level. Alice was a little disappointed that Clyde was not enjoying the music too. It was a rare and delightful scene to be sure. After all, how can people at various stages of Alzheimer's Disease be exactly in sync at the exact same time? She contemplated the answers. It almost seemed staged or programmed.

Alice found herself in front of apartment 29. She stood for a moment, listening. It was very quiet. No light was shining from under the door. No sense of any movement at all. "Perhaps he's taking a nap," she mused. Nurses Bill and Dorothy were rounding the corner to do a safety check on Doctor Abrainium. "How is Doctor Abrainium this morning?" queried Alice. "I noticed that he did not join everyone for our morning social engagement. Could you give me a report on his morning so far?"

"Doctor Abrainium is doing very well," said Dorothy. "He and I had a delightful conversation about an hour ago right before he indicated that he wanted to take a nap. We joined him for breakfast on his patio. He passed along his compliments to our chef saying how very good everything was. He was all ready to go out before we arrived. He changed his mind about going out for breakfast and invited us to stay with him instead. His Robot, Levi, reported that no environmental interruptions or issues occurred during the last twelve hours. We verified this report and noted that his vitals have been consistently stable throughout the entire period."

"They remain stable even now as he sleeps," offered Bill as he was checking his wristband monitor. "That is good news. I am relieved to learn of this as I was a little concerned not to see him out this morning with everyone else." I must say that you all did a fantastic job to gather all residents at once and keep them engaged this morning for the music. They all are having a terrific time! It is truly marvelous. When I noticed that Doctor Abrainium was missing, I wanted to check on him. It has been an interesting morning. Such a joy to see!"

Dorothy smiled warmly back at Alice. "Doctor Abrainium is just having a nap now?" Alice motioned with her hand toward his door.

"Yes." Bill answered.

Alice added "I don't really wish to disturb him if he's sleeping, but I am quietly going to just peek in on him to make sure he's OK. His two sons and grandchildren are all visiting him later this afternoon to start the program. I want to make sure that he is up for it."

"Wait! Bill exclaimed. "Before you check in on Dr. Clyde, Ms. Alice, Dorothy and I want you to know our thoughts. We have observed that even though Doctor Abrainium has been here for about seventy-two hours, his cognition has improved since arriving. It has gotten better. Yes, he has wonderful and witty conversations with us. He is cognitively aware of his surroundings the time and date and quite able to indicate this to us. He completely takes care of himself. He questions us. So, we are questioning, Miss Alice, if Doctor Abrainium really belongs here with us.

Alice was listening as she put up her left index finger while nodding her head yes. As if to say, 'I hear you and I will talk to you about it in just a minute.' Alice gently knocked on the door to his living area which was all dark and very quiet. She turned to Dorothy. "Please wait right here for me. I will talk to you in a minute after I go check on Doctor Abrainium." Alice tiptoed through the calmly decorated living area to his bedroom door. She noticed that Ellie robot was in her docking station as she should be. Turning to the doorknob slightly while gently applying pressure Alice loudly whispered his name "Doctor Abrainium? "Dr A?" No response. "It's Alice. The administrator. May I come in?" No response. "Doctor

Abrainium? It's Alice. Is it ok to come in?" Still, nothing. Alice gently opened the door a little more as her concern for him grew. Peeking in, expecting to see Doctor A. sound asleep on his bed. Her eyes adjusted to the dark room focusing on the queen size bed in full view then darted from one side of the room to the other. "Doctor A.?" Alice's voice was louder as she entered the room. He was nowhere to be seen. The bed was made. Had it been slept in? Alice looked all around. On the floor and in each room. If he got up or lost his balance Ellie sure would have detected it and let us know immediately. There were no messages. All was functioning as it should be. She would have reported it in real time so a nurse could respond and check. Alice thoughts were racing. She was a little confused but had her own theory about what she had come across this morning given what happened last night. Moving toward the bathroom door calling out his name and knocking. "Doctor A.? Doctor A.? Are you in there?" No answer came back. Alice's eyes were adjusted to the dark, however, she decided to turn on some lights. Alice announced that she was opening the door. Waiting for a response to which there was none. She opened the door to another empty room and turned on the light. Alice felt her blood pressure rise and her heart was racing. She took a deep breath and turned around to get Wil and Dorothy. As she turned toward the door, she came face to face with Doctor A. At the same time, Alice was distracted as she saw a bright light dart from across the patio door inside. It scared Alice.

Doctor A. was immaculately dressed in a suit. Alice guessed that his outfit was right out of the late 1960s or the early 1970s. He had headphones around his neck. Doctor A. quipped, "What is all the excitement about? It's like living at my son's house. Everyone is so worried all the time. I thought that I would have more peace and quiet here truly."

Bill and Dorothy were standing a few feet behind Doctor A. at this point. Alice was well aware of why her staff would have questions about Dr. A.'s cognitive abilities and his need to be here at Greenbrier Gardens. Doctor A. added, "I was just sitting in my back garden, enjoying my visit with my wife, Emily. I would love to have a full visit with my wife without being interrupted."

Bill and Dorothy looked at each other and back over at Alice with questioning looks. They could offer no explanation for this, so they both stayed quiet. They both knew that it was impossible for him to have visited his wife, Emily. They were familiar with his profile and had learned his life history. They knew that Emily had passed away over seven years ago. Alice looked at Doctor Abrainium's face and offered an apology. "I am so sorry that I disturbed your visit, Doctor Abrainium. It was not my intention to intrude upon your privacy. However, I missed seeing you at the music room this morning. I thought that I would check on you. See if you'd like to join us to visit the horses today.

"Horses? Oh yes. I would love to do that." Doctor A. exclaimed. "Emily loves horses Alice." She noticed that

Doctor's speech related to Emily in the present tense. Alice turned her attention to her staff. "It's alright Tod and Dorothy. Thank you for your diligence. Allow me a moment with Dr. Abrainium. We will be along shortly.

Will and Dorothy smiled back at them as they exited. Alice turned back around to focus again on Doctor A. She noticed he was clutching a small wooden object or box of some kind in his left hand. When Doctor A. saw her eyes look toward his hand, he nonchalantly gripped it more firmly. Alice looked away, recognizing that whatever it was he had there, must be something quite meaningful for him to try and hide it. She decided not to ask him about it. Instead, she asked him about Emily and the horses. Alice's demeanor reminded him of his Emily. That same gentle spirit and determination. A noble heart and always wanting to do the right thing. He heard Alice ask, "Do you like horses as much as Emily did?"

He responded, "Oh, I do like horses. But Emily loves horses. She loves all animals really. A gentle free spirit she is. No one could love horses more than she does."

"Well, that is happy news then. Are you ready to go meet our horse friends at the stable this morning Doctor A.?"

"Give me a moment to change my attire, please," Doctor A. said.

"Yes. Of course. I'll wait for you in the corridor and we can join the others. That OK?" Alice asked.

Will and Dorothy were also waiting patiently outside the door. Alice stepped outside into the hallway to greet them. I am not sure what just happened. he was sleeping, all reports indicated such," Will explained.

"Well for now if you could please but why don't you go and assist the other staff with the residents in the trip to the stables. Doctor Abrainium and I will be right there too, Will, see you shortly."

Alice watched as well, and Dorothy walked out of sight and around the corner. Alice replayed the recent scene in her mind putting him putting them in sequence the headphones music the 1970's suit the prop the small object in his hand the personal object shared by both things she learned from her husband Max that were necessary for time travel. That bright light Doctor A's moments of clarity. Then there was last night those voices I heard. I heard a woman's voice. Time travel but someone coming to this time. Doctor A is the one person that discovered the time travel platform he wrote the theory. Alice remembered reading about the three essential pieces that were necessary according to Doctor Abrainium, to facilitate time travel. The music of the era was important. You had to turn everything out and focus on music was important you had to be in costume you had to live in the moment you had to dress the part the last thing was something personal a personal object of some kind that was shared by you and the time traveler or the person that you were traveling to see something that represented both. Alice also remembered that all of that all of these were necessary to time travel, you must travel there in your mind. The molecular and magnetic change device in combination with the power of one's mind made the travel possible. You had to envision it first. You had to believe that it was possible as part of the preparation to travel. Then you turned on the device the device picked up your energy and then you traveled. Some rules apply she remembered Max explaining to her, sometimes though the time spirit of the person will follow you back. That may explain the woman's voice. That's where Doctor Abrainium's theory lost me Alice thought. Max will have to explain this to me Alice's thoughts raced ahead of her. What if we really could travel back and capture these residents' memories before their Alzheimer's disease onset. And use the MRP process to access those memories. They would keep their memories in order and sensibly. Their families loved ones would not lose them. Alice was excited about her thoughts and about the possibilities. But feeling somewhat suspicious and cautious more questions than answers about everything that last forty-eight hours. Perhaps Max could speak to Doctor Abrainium on his level and find out for sure what those missing pieces are.

"I'm ready to visit the horses now," Doctor Abrainium announced as he appeared in a pair of blue jeans and shirt, sneakers with a straw hat in hand. He smiled into Alice's eyes. "There is that look again," Alice thought. "That honest to goodness genuine smile that says, 'I have a wonderful secret that I wish I could share with you. Please ask me sincerely even if you dare.'"

"I am excited for you to meet Jack and Jane today, Doctor A. And the horses." Alice engaged in happy conversation with him on their way down the hall to meet up with the rest of the group.

Chapter 20: Sean and Uncle Neuman

Sean left his shift at 7:00 AM that Saturday morning. He headed straight to his Uncle Neuman's home studio as he had promised to do last night. "Uncle Neuman must have had some new important development to have me stop on the way home." Sean thought to himself. "I noted all my observations with Dr. Abrainium last night. I found a reason to dismantle Doctor Abrainium's robot, Waldo and harvested all recorded data. In review, I fail to see how this information will benefit Uncle in anyway. From what my uncle has shared with me about his work, this doesn't make much sense. How can one of our confused Alzheimer's residents contribute anything cohesive to this cause?" Perplexed, Sean pieced the events from last night in order in his mind to try to make some sense of all of this. All the while Sean was feeling more and more guilty about how he was sharing confidential information with his uncle. He was working at Greenbrier under a very strict code of ethics. He took an oath to uphold resident privacy dignity and confidentiality. He had certainly breached this trust already by traveling to his uncle's house and harvesting the information from robot Waldo. Alice had placed her trust in him. He had vowed to uphold this trust.

His heart was fighting with his mind, whispering with his logic on this point. Uncle Neuman had explained that if he could gather this last piece of information for him, he could finish his time travel theory. He would be able to help all the seventeen residents at Greenbrier Gardens. All the resident families would consider Uncle Neuman their hero. Alice and Max would be especially ecstatic.

"I am doing this to help these last seventeen victims of Alzheimer's Disease and heal their memories." Sean could hear his uncle's words. Sean continued to justify his actions mulling over his uncle's words. "If success is the result, I haven't done anything wrong. No one will find fault with how I obtained the information once they see what I have accomplished." Sean's uncle was quite convincing. "What could possibly go wrong?" his uncle asked him. "I only need this last piece from Dr. A. Sean. I guarantee that this will work. I will be taking care of you, Sean, I promise you." Sean knew what he was doing was wrong. But the pull of being family, he convinced himself that it will be all worth it and all will be forgiven. During that thirty-minute drive to his Uncle Neuman's house, he convinced himself that this was the right thing to do. "Let uncle Neuman finish this and now. Share it with the world. Make it a better place for everyone. Uncle Neuman would finally get the recognition that he deserved. I want to be like him someday to discover something important that will benefit humanity." Sean continued his thoughts. "No tasks should be left undone if for the betterment of all mankind." His uncle's words burned in his memory. He had always adored his uncle whom he deemed brilliant and passionate, yet under-noticed. Under-appreciated. Uncle Neuman is my family. I want him to succeed truly. Really what could possibly go wrong?" Sean asked himself. Sean's thoughts were reconciled with his heart now as he pulled into his uncle's laneway.

Chapter 21: Pony Days

Jane Lilly was completely delighted to be sitting atop her precious pony Dodi. Grandpa Max led her around the dirt track at the corner of the pasture. She loved these days. Horses and grandparents. The residents were obviously enjoying themselves also. Out in the fresh air sunshine the horses. They couldn't be smiling any bigger. There were seven horses and three ponies out by the fence this morning all wrangling for attention and some pets from the regular visitors outside of their fence. Each resident had a nurse companion, assisting and guiding them. Other staff members kept residents safe while they still felt free to be independent. Staff took care to make sure residents were dressed in appropriate attire, complete with long sleeve shirts, pants, sturdy closed toed shoes, hats and sunglasses. Sunscreen was amply applied while hydration stations in shady areas were strategically placed and plentiful. The residents talked to the horses. "Hello, pretty baby." "Beautiful!" The residents were delighted to pat the horse's heads and rub the horse's noses without fear. The horses communicated back to the residents in kind, showing their appreciation for the attention by bowing their heads to each other as well. Resident to horse in horse to resident. Some sort of telepathic language was exchanged that only they could understand. "What do you think of Prince Harry, Jack?"

Jack looked up at Doctor Abrainium to ask "Prince Harry?"

Doctor Abrainium responded? "Yes, this beautiful redhead as my mom calls him with his White Star on his nose. Oh, he's, my favorite. See how gentle and friendly he is. You can pet him like this." Jack demonstrated.

Alice was standing behind Jack and Doctor Abrainium snapping photos and videos to share with his family who could not be here this morning. Horse therapy sessions were very popular for their visitors. Alice was happy to see Sally's two daughters were here today visiting. Joe's son and granddaughter, James's age. Doctor Walters wife was here. And husband and daughter and grandson. Twenty-five visitors and all today. Staying for the picnic later too making smores old-fashioned sing along will complete the day's programs by about 6:00 or 7:00 PM. Residents are usually tired after a day like today and they sleep so well that's all part of the program get them to help them to sleep so well. Alice, really enjoying this scene, found her mind wandering back to the morning's events with Doctor Abrainium. She was so very anxious to discuss all of it with Max as soon as she could. But that would require complete privacy and she would have to be patient. Max could sense that Alice wasn't as calm as she usually is on these days there was something troubling her, he thought.

Max led Dodi with Jane proudly atop, to the fence where Jack and Doctor Abrainium were petting another pony, Harry. Alice motioned with her head for Max to move a little further down the fence. She wanted to say something to Max out of earshot of residents and visitors.

"You look a little distracted Alice. What happened this morning on your visit to Doctor Abrainium?" Max asked.

Alice replied in a loud whisper, "I need some time to fill you in on the details. At this point, I have more questions than answers, but I do have a theory. I can tell you that it has to do with time travel and Dr. A.'s visits with his wife."

"Time travel!" Jane Lily loudly blurted out. Jane's keen radar ears overheard her grandpa's words.

Max put his finger to his lips and looking at Jane, "Yes Jane. But it's a secret for now. What grandpa works on is a secret. Remember?"

"A secret. OK, Grandpa." Jane Lily whispered back.

Max gave his granddaughter a loving smile. Max and Alice turned their attention to the horses and their riders. "Such a glorious day!" Alice stated. She closed her eyes and took a deep breath. "Just what we all need more of. Days like this."

After some time in the fresh air and sunshine, the residents were getting tired. The nurse companions assisted the residents with some hydration before assisting them into the Mag Hover vans for their ride back to the main building. Taking their time, they enjoyed juice and fruit. The groomsmen took care of the horses, leading them back into the barn for their hydration too. The residents and their families were thoroughly enjoying this time together. Alice smiled as she observed how everyone interacted. Residents were calm and some were laughing. The horse interactions had a wonderful way of grounding the residents and Alice noticed that memories seemed to improve too. Carefree was the prevalent feeling hanging in the air. Once back at the main building, residents enjoyed a restful visit with their families out in the back garden with a barbeque. The staff stayed in the background, ready for any assistance that might be needed. Jack was enjoying an animated conversation with Doctor Abrainium and Mr. Henry, a retired police officer. Alice kept him in her eye's view, and kept Jane busy with her colouring and artwork at a table next to Jack's. Max pulled up a chair to join Alice and Jane, that was right next to Jack's chair. Alice was glad to have the time to explain the day's events, observations and her theory with Max. Alice shared the events of earlier that day, finishing with "I was also hoping that Doctor Abrainium might speak to you, scientist to scientist. What do you think? Perhaps he may shed some light on his visits with his wife. He may feel more comfortable with you, given your professional history together." Alice said. "I am convinced that his secret is that he travels back in time to visit his wife. He has it figured out Max."

Max responded, "After what I already know about him and my time travel theory, I am certain that you are right on the mark, Alice. Everything you observed. It all seems to fit. Doctor Abrainium is time traveling. This is so exciting! I believe he really is visiting his wife. I would like to perform an experiment to prove this theory. If I can do that, I will also be able to travel. I will bring my MRP with me. I will try visiting you, say in 1985. See if I can capture memories in real time with my MRP Alice! This could mean so much to helping your other residents!" Max continued, clearly in his own theory inspired world at this point. "I need to do a test though first. If all goes well, I will time travel next. This can be the way to help these last residents." Max was on cloud nine.

Alice listened to Max intently as she always did. She was concerned that this was all happening too soon. She felt that Max was jumping ahead and needed more time to practise his theories. She was afraid it could be dangerous if done too soon. Max continued, thinking out loud. "One resident at a time. It could prove to be a long process though, Alice. We will need to pinpoint the precise moment in time before the disease process set in for each resident and capture their memories with the MRP, to ultimately be successful." Max's voice took a more serious tone. "It is such a dangerous mission though. There are all kinds of people that would like to use this information and practise for no good. Alice, we cannot under any circumstances discuss any of this with anyone. Doctor Abrainium included. He shouldn't know that we have any idea about our own time travel theory and how close we are to travelling. We cannot discuss any of this with staff. It's all about time and making it precise. We will put our plan together, Alice. We can work with the families to gather each resident's disease process information with the consents and waivers necessary to move forward. We are so close, Alice. We will be successful! This will require some very careful strategy."

Chapter 22: Toronto

In Toronto, Adelaide and Thomas were having a wonderful and much needed weekend to themselves. The spa treatments, tennis matches, and fabulous dining experiences were dreamy. "Dreamy." Adelaide purred. "This is just what we needed." She gave Thomas a flirty smile.

"Yes, darling," Thomas agreed. "It will be great to see Will Henry and Beth tonight at dinner. To catch up with my brother and his fiancé. I can hardly wait! Find out all about what they've been going on and with them. I excited to find out about Beth's research project in Scotland. Yes, it has been way too long between visits, with almost a whole year passing.

Chapter 23: Missing in Action

"Alice, did Dr. Abrainium ever mention anything about the first time he met his wife, Emily?" Max asked his wife.

With a very sleepy little three-year-old girl resting her head on Nana's shoulder, Alice commented, "It's common knowledge that he met her on the fairgrounds of The Western Fair in London, Ontario, isn't it? They were waiting in line for a ride? He doesn't talk about dates. He talks about his experiences with his wife. I think we can research the answer for you." Alice offered as she gently placed Jane on a nearby couch. C"an you stay with Jack and Jane while I go back and check. Then we better get these two homes to bed."

Max took Jane Lily from Alice's arms and turned around to ask Jack to come along to sit down on a recliner and rest, they have had quite an eventful day.

Jack was nowhere in sight. "Max where is Jack he was just right here." Alice's voice was frantic. Max and Alice's eyes darted around the expanse of the large sitting room they were in. Residents were enjoying their family visits and relaxing, laughing, their nurse companions were close by.

"He was certainly enjoying chatting with Doctor Abrainium just moments ago with the horses. Doctor Abrainium's family left a little while ago. Perhaps that's where he is. Let me go check Dr. A.'s home and see if that's where they are."

Max decided to follow Alice, all be it slower with a sleepy Jane Lily resting on his shoulder. The door to Dr. A.'s home was open. Alice was relieved to hear her grandson's voice coming from within. "When will you be returning Doctor Abrainium? I know my grandmother and your family would be very worried if you are not here." Jack's young voice was so concerned. "Only my grandfather can time travel. I'm not allowed to go or even talk about it."

A flushed faced Alice was now standing beside her grandson. "Doctor Abrainium?" she asked.

"He's gone Nana. Doctor Abrainium said he was going home to see Emily."

"Oh, my great goodness!" Alice whispered to herself. "Jack's in here," Alice called back to Max.

"Grandpa, did you know that Doctor Abrainium can time travel just like you?" He questioned. "He did just now he's gone he's gone to visit Emily." Alice and Max's eyes met each other's; no words were spoken. They each knew what had to happen now what had to happen next. Alice was worried about Clyde.

Jack looked up at his grandmother. "Yes, we were all worried, Nana. But he said he would be back in time for his bedtime."

"Max darling, can you please take the children home now. I will stay here, and I will wait until Doctor Clyde has returned safely. I know that that might take a long time I'm not sure when I'll be home. I was hoping there were other explanations for his behavior though this is so concerning on so many levels."

Max offered some comfort to Alice, "Well it also explains the other experiences that you were having Alice. Like I said I really believe by everything that you've told me that Doctor Abrainium is certainly time traveling the robot, Waldo, shows experience and behavior I think they're all related we need to find out what's going on and make sure that everything's on the up and up, Alice. I'll take the children home and I look forward to seeing you back home soon you know Doctor Abrainium certainly wasn't hiding the fact from any of us remember Alice.

"He told us the first afternoon that I met him, Max, that if he can visit Emily every day or every night it doesn't really matter where he lives. His son shared that this was the reason he had to come here and asked for my help. They said that their dad was speaking nonsense visiting their mom daily after she been gone for seven years. It all makes sense in a strange way. Well please be safe please keep him safe dear God."

Alice sent up a prayer on his behalf." Come along Jack, Grandpa is going to take you and Jane Lily home now. Thanks darling, I really appreciate it. I will keep you posted." She leaned up to give him a kiss goodbye. "Goodnight Jane." She gently kissed her on the head wiping the hair out of her eyes. Bending down to Jack, "Thank you for trying to keep Doctor Abrainium safe. You are such a sweet and good-hearted young man, Jack. Nana loves you very much." Alice kissed Jack on the cheek. "I will be home before you know it."

Chapter 24: Beggar's Banquet

Max turned out the light in the children's room as they both drifted off to dreamland. Max had everything he needed to travel. He checked off all the boxes for the sixth time, music of the area of the arrow, check, clothing, costume, check, the date, the time, the event, checks, the transmitter programmed chat buttoning up the silky long sleeved orange Paisley shirt. Max looked in the mirror for a full effect. Wow, I mean, holy cow, Max exclaimed to himself. So, this was considered the wear of the 1970s this was cool? Max reviewed his look. Polyester dark tan pants with a longer style jacket to match. Ankle brown leather boots two-inch heels completed his ensemble. Max ran through the study material from the era. History up to then. Common sayings. Even had what was the common current currency of the era, cash bills, coins, all from 1969 or earlier. Brown leather wallet held the currency along with a few pieces of ID. Also researched to duplicate as closely as possible. An Ontario driver's license and sim card Anna library card. Specific notes about Doctor Abrainium in the event he was planning on attending the lyrics and music to song from The Guess Who, Marvin Gaye and John Denver played in his mind can you dig it let's boogie don't be such a grody, dream on, far out. all researched sayings from the era. Yes, Max had well researched this era, the movies, popular songs, food, the sayings, the television, the fashion and of course, the history. The entire decade as well as the 1960s history downloaded onto a small transmitter attached to the back of his right ear. he had a small bag packed too. Max would be staying at the Moonlight Motel throughout his trip and although he hoped that his trip would be only twenty-four hours or less, he was prepared to stay up to seventy-two hours. His transmitter was secured while two MRPS were adhered to his calves for safekeeping through the time travel process. Yes, Max believed he was ready to travel. he had done his research taking everything he needed to be time travel prepared. What he couldn't believe, as he glanced at himself in the mirror, was that people dressed like this back then. The music was catchy though. Max thought to himself. No cell phones, Internet, robots or teletherapy back then. Atari? The digital camera, the Sony Walkman. But the cat scan wasn't invented until 1973 I'm traveling to 1971, I can't even talk about cat scans I have to be careful. The Star Wars movie series, that cult popular series didn't start until 1977. I can't talk about that either. 1971 movies Max thought to himself *Willy Wonka and the Chocolate Factory* with Gene Wilder. *Shaft. Dirty Harry* with Clint Eastwood. *The Last Picture Show*. Billy Jack. *The French Connection. The Summer of 42. Bed knobs and Broomsticks. Planet of the Apes. Play Misty for Me*. With Clint Eastwood again? All this information was in Max's ear. All this significant music, 1970's culture, fashion, historical events downloaded into this tiny chip behind my ear. These were significant in Clyde's life too. I wonder what kind of music he listened to. All this information was captured on this microchip to be retrieved later when prompted by my thoughts in my will. Well, to the western fairgrounds I go, the fall of 1971 London, yes here I come Max said to himself. Orange Paisley shirt, polyester pants and all.

Chapter 25: Dr Abrainium Confesses

Alice turned toward doctor A's voice. It had been almost two hours since Max took the children home. Alice had been patiently waiting for Doctor A's return. She was trying not to panic about his sudden absence. Quotation even with all our technology to show that Doctor A was still on our premises, he managed to manipulate it and leave us another way. "Doctor A," Alice's voice sounded relieved. "We were all so worried about you! I'm so happy to see you." Alice searched Doctor A's face and his eyes for his recognition of this fact.

Doctor A stammered, "You know where I go at night Alice."

"Yes, I do, and I completely understand. And I'm so impressed by you beyond belief, Doctor A. that you can time travel. You've lived and you are the living proof of your own theory."

"Yes Alice. And I have discovered that even in my backwards travel I cannot change the time I cannot change the events. I am merely a spectator in time as they happen. I miss my wife Emily so very much and this is the only way that I can be with her. See her, talk to her."

Alice's big, brown, kind eyes told Doctor A that she really did understand. Her heart was heavy for him without saying a word. Doctor A continued, "My memories of Emily, of our life together are fading now. They present in pieces in my mind. It's happening more and more now. I am afraid I'm losing her in her memory. I do know she's gone now. But even my memories of her are getting lost. I'm having difficulty retrieving them. Traveling back is the only way to help me remember her. Emily loved music. She loved to dance." He smiled. "My mind itself, my memories I seem to be stuck in and they are stuck in a time warp. As I said it's happening more quickly, and I know that I will not be able to travel back anymore soon. It's dangerous to bring her time spirit back with me to here to the now."

Alice was speechless. She could not imagine what it would be like to lose her Max. To lose the memory of him too. She could feel his loss, "I am so sorry Clyde. I would like to hear more about Emily."

Doctor A. was sitting down in his recliner. Once again Alice was reminded that although Doctor A. was lucid at this moment, in the next, he may not be. He looked so very tired. Drained. He was declining and may not make another time travel trip she thought. "You look like you need to take your adventures and memories to dreamland now Doctor A," Alice offered.

Doctor A was sleepy. His night nurse companion, Jennifer, gently knocked at the door to see if everything was all right if there's anything that she could do. It had been over two hours since Jennifer knew that Alice had come to visit Doctor A. after all Jennifer thought. "Oh, please do come in Jennifer,"

Alice responded. Jennifer entered with a tray filled with various cut fruit pieces, biscuits, juice and she placed it on the kitchen counter. "Doctor A. had quite an eventful day, Jennifer. Thank you for assisting him tonight."

Doctor A. really liked Jennifer. She was kind and sweet. She listened to his stories, and she had a few of her own too. Jennifer knew exactly what his favorite treats were. Although there was no chocolate on that tray, he could be sure that there was a piece or two in her pocket. As Alice was leaving Doctor A. said loudly, "Neuman," he repeated, Neuman something about Neuman September 10th, 1971. Alice caught the confused look on Jennifer's face. Jennifer had already gotten familiar with doctor A's time travel stories.

Doctor A. was sharing stories with me," she said.

Alice was also really concerned about the comment that Doctor A had just made, she wondered what he was trying to tell her. "Goodnight, Doctor, A." Alice said. "You are in good hands now." As she stepped outside, Alice mulled over the information Doctor A. had provided. September 10th. Interesting. Nothing significant could come to her mind, though. The date combined with the Neuman comment stuck in her mind. Alice knew Doctor Neuman didn't know Doctor A. It was quite perplexing. Alice texted Max and added the message "Neuman September 10th, 1971."

Chapter 26: The Trip

Max was cautiously excited about his imminent trip to 1971. He had his concerns. After his successful simulated time travel trials this would be his first real trip. His thoughts were interrupted by someone's voice. "Dad. Where are you?" He recognized his daughter's voice. "Adelaide? Yes. I'm here. Come on up."

Adelaide dashed up the stairs with her husband Thomas at her heels. "Look who we bumped into, Dad." At this point all the most precious people in his life were standing right before him. Max was elated. "Will It's so good to have you home!" Max exclaimed as he gave his son a big hug. "And Beth!" He turned and offered her a big hug too. With tears brimming he said "I can't believe it you're all here this is such a joyous occasion! Just wait until your mother gets here! She will be beside herself with happiness! It's just been too long!" Max was so excited to see all of them he didn't notice the questioning looks all of them had on their faces. Particularly his son.

"Peace. Yeah. Groovy, Dad." Will laughed.

"Yeah. Can you dig it?" Adelaide played along continuing to rib their dad.

"Look Dad I don't know what you're into right now but if you and Mom need some space..."?

"Oh! No," Max jokingly responded. "You are referring to my manner of dress this evening?"

"Yes," Will said.

"With that orange paisley shirt. What's up with that?"

"My goodness! Those shoes are a trip, Dad."

Adelaide interjected "What's going on here? A back in time party?"

"That's a bit of a story. Let's go downstairs and sit down together. I will explain." Max said, motioning to the door.

"We will be right along, Dad." Thomas said. "I want to check in on Jack and Jane first."

Max put his arm on his son's shoulder. Looking in Beth's direction, Will said "This should be good, Beth. My dad always has some time experiment he's working on."

The whole family gathered in the kitchen. Max opened the fridge. Turning to look at them, "What will it be everyone? Some wine? Milk? Juice? Water? It's vintage. Well? We should celebrate. It's not every day that we are all together." Max went about moving jars and bottles around in the fridge. "I think we still have a bottle of champagne here somewhere." Max bent over to look through the beverage compartment of the fridge.

"Oh! That sounds marvelous!" chimed Beth.

"A sip to success! A sip to celebrate!" "Are we having champagne?" Adelaide queried as she and Thomas breezed into the kitchen. She gave her dad a kiss on the cheek. "Jane and Jack have completely gone to dreamland. Thank you for taking such good care of them."

"Yes. We had quite an eventful day. Jane and Jack are all played out by now."

"Yes, we greatly appreciate it, dad."

"How much they love you too, dad," Thomas added. "What is it with this orange Paisley, I need to know where you are headed with this."

All four of them had their attention directed at Max as he placed six champagne flutes on the marble island, they were sitting at. "Your mom just texted me let's wait until she arrives, shall we?" Max offered.

Will was sure this was related to his dad's time travel theory that he had been working on. Max had kept his son quite aware of each step along the way in the process. They had a very strong bond of trust, and they bantered theories about periodically. They had developed this relationship ever since Will could walk and talk. Will was always right at his dad's side every waking moment learning as much as he could. His dad was the reason he pursued his triple doctorate degrees, the molecular biology degree in physics with the human engineering and the artificial intelligence. Max is so very proud of Will's accomplishments. But more so for his astuteness of character and pure heart. He was brilliant at absorbing information and developing his own theories they came so very naturally to Will.

Will had to cut to the chase though. "So, Dad, what are you doing? Are you taking a trip back to the 1970s then?"

Max was about to reply when Alice bounced through the back door and into the kitchen. "Oh, wow this is completely a wonderful surprise! I do not know what to say! Thomas Adelaide! We didn't expect you until tomorrow!" Alice said giving them both hugs. Turning to William and Beth, "And you are too! Oh well! It's so very wonderful to see you! I didn't think I would see you until November." Alice gave him a long embrace. "Beth, you look lovely as always, she said turning to her, giving her an extended hug too. Looking at the champagne flutes in the champagne bottle on the counter Alice said, "Oh we're about to have champagne? Yes?"

"Yes, we are celebrating just being together. And will have some big news for us I believe" declared Max.

Thomas offered to open the bottle." Pop. You can pour," Max is instructed.

"Well, dad, were you planning on a trip to 1971 tonight what's going on?" asked Will.

Everyone went quiet. All eyes were on Max, waiting for his reply. Max knew that his trusted close family knew all about his travel theory through time even though they were not quite sure the theory would ever prove to be a reality. Max simply answered, "Yes." Looking straight at his son in his eyes.

"OK, Dad. Then you can't go alone. I will go with you." Will's response was matter of fact.

Beth looked over her at her fiancé. "What?"

"You and I will forego the champagne then son. We can't drink champagne before we go on a time travel trip."

"Max. As I was leaving tonight, Doctor A repeated this to me," Alice interjected. "Neuman September 10th, 1971".

"Neuman? What on earth have could he have meant by that.

"I'm not entirely sure," Max said, "but what I am sure of is that Doctor A has been traveling through time and he was there tonight."

"Let's raise a glass then," Thomas suggested, "to 1971."

"To 1971," they all chimed in together.

"To memories, love, family," added Alice.

"Dad, do you happen to have another one of those shirts?" Will asked.

"Funny you should ask, son," Max replied.

Will and Beth decided to wait to share their celebratory news.

Chapter 27: Travel Rules

"I understand you have successfully sent the artificial intelligence back and brought them back several times. I have faith that this trip will prove successful and will pave the way for more." Will said to his father. "I understand the purpose of this trip is to help Doctor Abrainium. This process is the beginning to also help the other sixteen residents that live at Greenbrier Gardens."

"Yes. Will. You are correct. I hope that future time travel will prove easier after this maiden trip, Will. So, with that, you are in then?"

"You bet, Dad. I'm in."

"Time to review the travel rules, Will." Max replied.

"I think I have them by now, Dad. You have been teaching me ever since I can remember."

"Rule #1." Max went right into his rules as if he didn't hear his son. "You cannot change events in the past as an attempt to change the future or the present. This is extremely important and a delicate balance. you cannot use knowledge of the future to change events in the past further you cannot bring knowledge from the past to the future to change anything either, this includes knowledge of any technology to help someone. Rule #2, do not become emotionally involved with anyone or discuss or communicate with anyone for any reason in the past that you are visiting. Rule #3 remember the era that you were in and fit in. Wear the ear chip that will always give you the information for the era that you are visiting. Rule #4 if we become separated, we must meet at the exact same place and the same time of day that we landed. If we travel in together, we must travel back together. Rule #5 make sure that you always carry with you those three essential pieces, the music piece, the memory piece, the artifact and stay in character and in costume.

Will was standing next to his dad in his lab. "You understand the mission of this trip will?"

"Yes, I got it, Dad. Beth Adelaide Thomas and Alice, we're all there to say goodbye.

"Your blue and violet flowered shirt is simply breathtaking, Will," Beth added.

"It must be possible, Doctor A. has done this several times it seems and always returns," said Alice.

"Oh yes," they all agreed a little bit hesitantly they weren't so sure that they were saying goodbye to their dad and brother for the last time.

"I'm more than ready," Max said.

"Yes, let's take a trip back to 1971, Dad."

Beth and Will said their goodbyes. Max and Will had their three essentials. they had their time guide amulet which was their ticket home too. With everything in place now Will and Max were ready to say goodbye to their loved ones and ready to walk through the time portal to 1971 leaving 2042 and their family behind.

Chapter 28: 1971

Noise. Laughter. 1971 music. Small and large crowds of people, couples, families everywhere. In lines for rides. The smells filled the air. Popcorn. Hot dogs. Burgers. Fries. Food on sticks. Cotton candy. The click click click of the chains taking the four person carts up to the tall climb to the very top of the rollercoaster before the mouse cart dropped them down to the bottom in seconds. "That is completely wild, Dad," offered Will. Looking up at the mouse ride. "Did you ever ride that thing, Dad? I cannot believe that we are here. I mean, here, I need to pinch myself this is really 1971."

"I know, we did it," Max exclaimed excitedly.

"That wasn't an easy walk though, Dad, I was wondering about, it was touch and go and then everything went dark, and I lost sight of you. I'm just so glad that we got here safely."

"Well let's get started to find Clyde he's supposed to be here tonight at nineteen years old and Emily is supposed to be here too. let's have a look at their older photos again."

Both Will and Max took a moment to survey their surroundings. Will patted his pockets to make sure that everything was still intact and secured. "How do I look?" Max asked Will.

"You look exactly as you did when we left 2042, Dad. And judging by the look of another gentleman here tonight I would say that you fit right in." Will laughed out loud. "How about me?" Will asked. "Is my hair still in place?"

"You fit right in here as well, Will Henry," his dad replied to him. "Let's see. There is a locker area to place our bags in until we find Doctor Abrainium should we need them. We will keep an eye out for Doctor Abrainium as well on our way over to the lockers. Bring his 1971 image up."

"Got it," Will said, a nineteen-year-old Clyde's facial image appeared in the left side of Will's contact lens it was generated from the memory chip implanted behind his right ear. Max did the same they now knew exactly who they were searching for. Doctor A. described in quite detail the day that he met Emily. "It was right here on this day sometime in the late afternoon. Could have been anytime between 3:00 PM and 5:30 PM. Well, it's 1:43 PM now. So, we have a few minutes to put our bags in the lockers and come back." Clyde's words from his own diary leapt from the page and was also in front of both will and Max for them to read so they understood the circumstances of their first meeting. "What should we do next?" Nancy asked.

"Let's go over there," suggested Emily as she motioned over to some young men standing in front of a ride. "Today I met an extraordinary young woman," Clyde said, "quite lovely although somewhat reddish long wavy hair. Cheeky young lady with flashing green eyes. I noticed that she was with four of her friends. However, she approached me alone and struck up a conversation which was the cheeky part. My friend Bob was equally puzzled why such a very lovely young lady would do this."

Emily said to her friends, "Look at that guy over there he is so cute!" Emily's younger sister, fifteen-year-old Kay, just rolled her eyes. Nancy, Tina and Jill looked across the dirt ground about fifty yards away to size up the boys Emily was referring to.

"Do you want to just go stand over there close to those guys Emily?"

"Yes. We will get in line for the for the ride and see if they will notice us." The girls were always looking at boys. The girls looked at each other somewhat skeptically though questioning.

"Oh OK, let's go," Nancy said. Although they looked deep in conversation the two young men did look in the direction of the girls in the end of the ride line. "Don't look so obvious Emily," implored Nancy. As Emily scampered ahead to get in line. Emily noticed him right away as she turned around and surveyed the area. She wanted to decide what ride they should go on next when her eyes rested on him, he glanced up from his conversation. Their eyes met. Time stood still for one long minute. Emily was the one to look away first. The two young men continued their deep conversation when the five young lady friends landed in the middle ride line just a few feet from them. Emily turned around to see if he noticed her. I wonder what they can possibly be discussing so deep in conversation for this long. Emily asked herself. here at the fair. Emily did not see Clyde look up from his conversation. Bob's back was where Clyde's glance was directed so he turned also look. "What is it that you are so distracted with," Bob questioned.

He looked at his friend and turned around, "Oh I see, yes; she is quite striking, but we are here for a different purpose Clyde, I remind you. We need to focus on the next steps of why we're here," Bob reminded Clyde. "If you want to continue with your theory and become a doctor, you'll have no time for any type of relationships. You just won top science innovation award for your theory."

"You're quite right Bob. As I said I am very intrigued with the thought of being able to travel through time yet even for a physician major it is it is seemingly so far-fetched." Clyde was refocused on Bob's words. And he was facing Bob listening, yet his thoughts were still thinking about the young woman who stood in the middle of the ride line just a few feet away. "Well to help demonstrate my theory I think we ought to take a ride on this wild mouse roller coaster," Clyde excitedly suggested.

Bob's eyebrows furrowed together and raised. "I fail to see how that will help me understand anything," Bob stopped midsentence as it became very apparent why they were both standing in line suddenly for this ride. I do hope we don't stand in line much longer K fast. She was impatient and as she turned around to check out what was going on her eyes locked briefly with Clyde's.

A little embarrassed Kay turned back around and leaned toward her older sister. Whispering, "Don't turn around that guy you think is so cute is now standing in line right behind us." Emily's heart sped up a little and she felt a hot flush consume her whole body. Emily responded to Kay. "Get a hold of yourself, Emily,". she said to herself. she couldn't seem to help herself though. there was just something about this young man that she was attracted to and could not explain. She was so drawn to him. Emily took a minute and casually turned around to pretend to look at something off in the distance to see if this young man was indeed standing behind them. He was looking straight at her when she turned around. She realized that he was right there she glanced away quickly. Nancy and the girls were engrossed in another conversation about their coming up senior year in their high school. To Emily it was distant chatter. A sophomore next year Kay was only halfway paying attention. Kay was much more interested in keeping an eye on her older sister. She's behaving a little strangely right now Kay said to herself. Kay was surprised to see Emily turn around and move past the young family waiting in line behind them to get in line. The only barrier between the two young men and themselves. Emily moved toward Clyde. Her eyes locked in a gaze with him as she stood right in front of him. "Hello I'm Emily." she said. she felt compelled to take this opportunity to introduce herself although her heart was racing. Well hello Emily Clyde responded my name is Clyde. And this is my friend Bob nodding towards Bob. I am happy to meet you. Have you ridden on this rollercoaster before Clyde asked. Oh yes, many times it looks kind of scary but it's really a lot of fun. Have you she asked no this will be my first roller coaster ride here. Well would you like to accompany me on this ride since you're the experienced one he asked I understand the limit is 4 riders per cart Clyde's eyes shifted to look at Emily to Emily's right Emily turned to see what he was looking at Kay was standing right there too. I'm K Anne I am her sister she interjected. And my dad will not like it that my sister is talking to a couple of strangers. And a man stranger at that. Kay exclaimed. I quite understand Kay. Clyde added this is my friend Bob we are students at the University of western Ontario and are here for the science exhibits. In Clyde here won top honors for his physics innovative theory category. Is that right Kay was immediately intrigued. Kay looked at her sister and then back to Clyde. They sure seem to like each other already staring each other like that Kay thought to herself come on Emily let's go back with Nancy Tina and Jill we've got to get on the ride. It was nice to meet you Emily Clyde said. Look me up in the physics Department sometimes I am Clyde Abrainium. Emily. Emily Cameron. Emily yelled back at Clyde. Emily Cameron of Thorndale. Kay started pulling her away. The next ride had emptied out as they were standing there and had begun to seek groups of three or four in each next car. The girl stepped aside to allow the family of four to go next. As they waited in line Nancy said "well there's five of us. You Jill and Tina go on the next cart anion Emily will take the next one K suggested. The next car was there the three took their seats and strapped themselves in all set the ride conductor yelled. We're next K squealed. As Kay got into her seat Emily turned around to see another glance to take another glance at Clyde. At that moment Clyde handed Emily a small, folded piece of paper which Emily smiled and stuck into her tucked into her back Jean pocket quickly just in time before Kay could notice..."

Chapter 30: Capturing Memories

"Were you able to capture that entire episode, Dad," Will asked.

"Yes, I was able to do that fun and in real time. I just can't believe we made it here all in time to capture these moments in real time, Dad."

"I was somewhat nervous about this," Max replied, "Incredible! Virtually an undisturbed moment in time this is so exciting. "Remember, son, we are all merely time bystanders. Do not stop to speak to anyone. Do not impede the activity happening around you in any way possible. It is imperative that we in no way engage ourselves in conversation or anything that could change history in the future in any way we need to tread lightly, son."

"We were able to accomplish this task, Dad, I'm so excited."

Just as Max finished speaking, he looked around to see if anyone even noticed their presence. "Neuman!" Max, his voice was slow and disbelieving.

Will looked towards where his dad was looking and asked "Well that looks like Neuman over there talking to that man. The one who is with Doctor Abrainium. I think his name is Bob. I can't believe it. Is that really Neuman?"

asked will, "What is he doing here and how did he get here what is going on?

"Well, we need to find out right now," Max said a little disturbed and upset. "I don't know how or why he's here, but we must speak to him immediately and find out what's going on with him. He must need to get back to the year 2042 and soon he's going to disrupt history. He could cause a lot of damage. Let's go, son.

"How are we going to accomplish that, Dad?

Max is walking very fast around the ride to where Neuman was hoping he would not be detected until he could get right in front of him and confront him and Will was right on his heels

Chapter 31: What Neuman Knew

Neuman knew that he was taking a huge risk embarking on this trip. He had collected everything that he needed to travel. Everything that he had learned from Dr. Abrainium's experience in the information. He had everything to travel back to 1971 to meet Doctor Abrainium and intercept that moment in time when Doctor Abrainium had his time travel theory. He could grasp that theory. The moment in time when Dr. Abrainium met Emily. Neuman needed this first and most important piece to the time travel process. He could then indeed claim his theory in process as his own. He would have the fame. The notoriety. He would have the money. He deserved this. His family, his history, claimed back. Neuman pondered his plan as he did a final check of what he had to take for this trip. The time monocular device as well as cash money from the 1968 to the 1970 era. He had a microchip with photos of Doctor A and his family, close friends of Emily, their history, all downloaded into this tiny chip behind Neuman's right ear. He was so thankful that his nephew had been able to retrieve all the specific information dates and times with events to pinpoint the destination so that he could use it. He took one last glance around and a deep breath looking in the mirror. I guess I look like I felt I was in 1971 wearing a subdued green blue and beige polyester suit with a plaid blue shirt. Brown ankle boots with two-inch heels I don't know what they were thinking back then Neuman mused to himself. Neuman had also just decided that for expediency that he would do no test trips back he was so confident in his ability she just wanted to go back to 1971 and get on with his plan. Neuman had the small TM CD monocular change device with him as well as everything in his pocket when he did the last check once outside, he began walking down the sidewalk, he needed to be in motion to make the time travel work he knew that much. He placed his palm on the device taking another deep breath he disappeared into the cityscape down the sidewalk

Chapter 32: What Max Knew

Max knew that he had no way to magically send Neuman back to 2042. He knew that he would have to convince Neuman that it was the right thing to do. Neuman should not be talking to anyone in this time or be involved in any way. Max was furious. It was extremely dangerous of him to do this. He had so many questions in his mind about Neuman and how he got there and why he was here. Max knew that they would all be stuck in 1971 if Neuman did anything or involved himself in anything it could cause them to be stuck there in this time. Neuman was immersed in this conversation with Bob but felt a presence and compelled to look around and look up. His jaw dropped when he saw Max's tall imposing figure standing right in front of him. Neuman was speechless. Bob saw the shocked look on his new friend's face and turned to see who Neuman was looking at.

"Neuman." It was Will's voice." Good to see you here, we have something important to talk to you about." Will continue towards Bob, "Hi I'm Will, and this is Max, excuse us for a moment please."

"Oh, of course, nice to meet you both," Bob replied. "I'll see you all later at doctor's lab tomorrow then,"

Neuman nodded, "Yes." Bob bowed out.

Will had a difficult time trying to keep his emotions in check, he was so angry with Neuman. "Neuman, what in the devil do you think you are doing? Why are you here and how did you get here? What in the blazes do you think you're doing? How do you even know Will,'''' Max interrupted.

"Neuman what are you doing? What you are doing is so dangerous and I think you're aware of it I must say."

Neuman responded, "The same could be said about both of you, your appearance here. On some sort of time travel mission, are you? I know what you were going to say to me. I am also on a mission. I have just as much right to be here on my mission as you do on yours and I have a very important one at that.

Really Max was disbelieving. "You know that speaking to anyone in this time era could do irreversible damage to the future and to the past period. Alter the course of people's lives and change them forever. You must come back with us now to avoid any more damage than what you could have already caused.

"I don't think so," Neuman said. "I have not completed what I came here to do." Neuman responded. Looking straight in the eye he would not back down. He knew what he had to do. Changing the future was why he was here he wanted to change the future and Max was not trying to change the future.

"Look, Neuman," Mx said, "we're all here to just capture one moment in time and we've done that, and we've done it quickly. Without contact or involvement with anyone. We need to get on our way back now you need to come with us. Please, Neuman, before more damage happens to the future. We all want to go back to our families just as we left them. They are waiting for us to return in 2042."

"Yes, my fiancé Beth," Will offered.

Max took the quick look at his son surprised, "Oh, son, really that's wonderful news. Congratulations you two got engaged I didn't know."

"Oh just stop," Neuman shouted, interrupting them. "You have everything to go home to! You have your family your children your grandchildren your happy home I have none of that! It was all taken from me such a long time ago and you know Max! My parents my sister I have no one! I'm here to change all of that. And I deserve to have what you have too. I was destined to win the award for the time travel process I almost had it. If I can change doctor a thought process if I can get the information from him if he never marries Emily, then my parents would never have died I would have this final piece to make it reality. My family would not have died in that car accident. I would have my family back. I would take my rightful place in history. The time travel process would be all due to me." Tears had formed in Neuman's eyes. He was so emotional and not thinking logically.

Will searched his thoughts for just the right thing to say to help convince him that he did need to come back to 2042 before any more damage was done, he looked at

Neuman with sympathy. Max put his hand on Neuman's shoulder, "Let's all take a breather." He nodded to an empty bench in a quiet area under an oak tree on the fairground. Max and Neuman went over and sat on the bench. Will chose to remain standing allowing his father to take the reins on this conversation. Max truly felt deep sympathy for Neuman he had known him for so many years. "Neuman. I am truly sorry. I was there with you remember when you were young when that call came about your parents at school. You stayed with us for a while until your aunt was able to make living arrangements for you to live with her but this Neuman doing this. This won't bring your family back necessarily it may make things worse. It may make your future worse it will do damage to the future of unknown numbers of other people. Just think of the ramifications all the technology that has been invented all the cures that we have now it could all be for not for one stroke of a conversation that you have here today Neuman could change all of that please don't let that happen. It won't necessarily give you the fame or notoriety that you seek that piece also Neuman. This can only result in harm to our future and our present. We walk into the future bringing the present with us and leaving the past behind us. We need to leave this now and get back to 2042 where we all belong.

Neuman did listen but was losing his patience with both frustrated he said, "Well all of that is so easy for you to say. You have a present to go back to I don't I don't have a present I don't have a future. I must try to change it. And you are here to change the future of things too don't deny it. You are a disruptor too just by being here. You contradict yourselves gentlemen." Neuman's voice was louder and emotional, not exactly Neuman.

"We are not here to disrupt, we are not here to deliberately insert ourselves to change history we're here to capture a memory to help doctor Abrainium," Will chimed in."

"Well you are a good young man I know that you believe that," Neuman said.

"Look, we need to leave and as quickly as possible we're all in agreement that staying here any longer than we should, will certainly change and impact history and perhaps not in a good way. Come on, Neuman, let me help you. Give me your TM CD let's all go together."

Max stood up and offered his hand to Neuman who also stood up and took Max's grip which surprised both Will and Max. Max and Neuman looked at each other. Quietly Neuman said, "I know you are right, Max. But you have wonderful memories I not so much. You have all those wonderful memories, well, your best memories could be yet to be made Neuman. You do have memories good memories of your mom and dad and sister you need to hang on to those Neuman.

"Yes, I suppose," Neuman said, "my parents used to come here to this fair too as teenagers I was hoping to see them," Neuman said.

Max offered, "I suppose it wouldn't hurt to do a quick lap around the fair, look at how we used to live as long as nobody interrupts or says anything to anybody."

"They all looked at each other they couldn't believe that Max actually offered that suggestion and they looked around then they did start to laugh a little bit about how everyone used to dress. 'Just look at what everyone used to wear."

"They looked at each other as well and shook their heads, "Yes just look at us! I kind of like the music though Will added, 'I like that American woman by The Guess Who it was playing on the loudspeaker overhead.

"Yeah, I agree," Neuman added smiling. "There was some cool music back then."

Dusk was coming upon them now, the neon lights lit up the sky. The ringing of bells, guesses your weight, could be heard in the distance. The roar of the roller coasters filled the sound space left after the music. Yes, popcorn smells cotton candy hot dogs fried grease smells permeated the air. Long lines were still forming at the food booth and at the rides. The fair attendees were all hustling around and bustling this way and that, laughing, happy, discussing what ride to go on next or what fried food they were going to try next. "Everyone looks to be happy here," Max observed as he looked around. Max recognized the song on the loudspeakers as one that they played often at Greenbrier Gardens. The absence of our modern-day technology making life so much simpler Max thought to himself. I wonder how they survived without all of it. Yet they did. "Come on Neuman and just take a few minutes on our way back to the travel site perhaps Neuman will get a glimpse of his parents."

Max did feel so badly for Neuman. But he needed to stay focused on their mission now that they had captured the memory getting back to 2042 was eminently important. Any destruction here in 1971 could impact their ability to get back if their presence interrupted their future. Max still had two more travels to complete for Doctor's MRP chip to activate it properly he had two more years to visit he planned on 1974 in 1978 as well. And now Neuman had messed that up for him he was going to have to reassess and re-calibrate what he was going to do to make sure that he had what he needed to help Doctor Abrainium

Chapter 33: Being Worried

Alice was worried. She certainly could not sleep. Max and Will had been gone now for several hours. She knew that it could be a couple of days before they got back but she couldn't help but worry. She went over the details of their trip in her mind. Max certainly had everything with him. He had pinpointed the exact location, date and time that Doctor A. had met Emily. Nex,t the exact location, date and time of their wedding. The birth of their children. 1971, 1974, 1978, already. "Mom." Addie's voice interrupted Alice's thoughts as she turned around to see her daughter entering the kitchen.

"Yes, Addie, you can't sleep either?"

"No not at all. I am quite troubled." Alice replied.

"I'm confident that Dad and Wil are going to walk right through that door any minute now." Addie replied.

"I am anxious."

"Perhaps a cup of tea? That always makes us feel better and calms us down."

Thunder clapped outside. Lightning flashed across the kitchen window. Suddenly it started to pour. Pouring the tea into her mom's cup, both Addie and Alice turned toward the squeals and the thump thump thump of small feet. "Mommy! The thunder is too loud!" Jane Lily cried.

"We can't sleep." Jack added. "Can we please stay up and have tea with you?" Jack pleaded.

"Please Nana?" Jane Lily chimed in, using her most convincing voice. Alice looked up at the old-fashioned clock to see that it was passed 10:00 PM already.

"It's up to your Mum. It's rather late you know." Just then an extremely loud clap of thunder hit the sky and made a long crackling sound. "OK. You two. just for a little while and then we need to get some sleep all right." Both children nodded.

Jane Lily squealed, "Yay," as she scooted up on a chair next to her Nana with her mom's help. Jack pulled up another chair for himself and preceded to get situated onto it.

"How about a little milk?" Nana asked them.

"Oh yes please," Jack and Jane Lily said in unison.

Alice got up to get each a glass of milk knowing that this was an unusual treat for Jack and Jane to stay up so late with the adults. Beth could not sleep either. Tossing and turning, she couldn't seem to get to dreamland. Beth was known in the family as the one who could sleep through anything. Thunderstorms usually didn't wake her up. She could usually sleep through even this loud thunderstorm tonight. And after the long trip from Africa here she was overly tired. The thought of Will and Max in a whole new world, and in a whole new time, 1971, was very unsettling to her made it difficult to sleep. Beth's usual calm demeanor gave way to anxiousness underneath. Springing out of bed, she decided to don her slippers and housecoat. Opening the door to the upstairs hallway she heard voices downstairs. Beth smiled to herself, two little voices chatting back and forth about thunderstorms. Addie and Alice laughing with the children. It was reassuring to Beth, and she loved to be here. She loved to belong. She could hardly wait to have Will back home and share these memories with him and share their news with everyone.

"Hello, everybody," she said. "Thunderstorms certainly have a way of gathering families together at odd times during the night," Beth offered as she greeted Addie Alice Jack and Jane.

"Oh Auntie Beth, we're having tea," Jane said excitedly.

"I would love to have some tea too," Beth said.

"How about me too?"

Oh, Thomas, you couldn't sleep either obviously. but Daddy," Jack or Jane chimed in.

"Well it certainly is a family affair tonight," and he laughed.

Thomas James a military physician and colonel in the army. Thomas was used to functioning with little sleep, given his profession but tonight was different. There was an electric energy permeating the air that had absolutely nothing to do with the storm outside. "Daddy the thunder is too loud," Jane Lily offered in her serious little three-year-old voice.

"It certainly is very loud I don't know if I have ever heard such a loud thunderstorm," he replied.

"And it even sound like it's knocking on the door," Jack said.

"It does indeed," Alice said.

Everyone went silent the second knock on the door was louder and much more earnest thump thump thump. "Who in the world—" Alice couldn't complete her sentence as Addie's somewhat nervous voice took over the conversation aiming her concern at her mom,

"I thought you had a secure perimeter here and surveillance warnings how could someone just have gotten past all of that and as far as our door?" Thomas, his voice was calm yet forceful. After his years of military training, he didn't mess around or miss a beat. "Please take Jack and Jane down the hallway to the safe space. Let's all stay calm," he said. "I think it's time for bed now kids. Why don't Mom and I take you the back to your bedroom," he asked

"OK, Daddy," Jane whispered as everyone else was quiet and her dad was speaking in a hushed tone.

Jack was already following his dad's lead and opened the back door over the kitchen that led through the safe hall to the safe room. As Addie bath and the children quickly exited the kitchen Alice was searching for the surveillance system that was built in to her IPS that she was wearing.

"You need to go too, Alice." Thomas offered. They had always had a high security on the premises due to the nature of Max's profession and what Alice did also.

"I can't see anything in my surveillance," she said. Perhaps this thunderstorm has had enough to knock down that part of our system to allow someone through the gate. I still have access to viewing the entire grounds in real time."

Thomas went closer towards the door on the other side of the kitchen, "No, wait, I see a small whitish gray hover vehicle no person is in it though, it looks like."

Alice said, "It looks like Sean's. We should answer the door."

"I know, I will answer the door," Thomas said, "Please take cover Alice."

Thump thump thump,

"I can't make who it is at the door, but I think it's I think it's Sean it is just one person, that much I can see.

"Sean yes, he is one of my IT engineers at Greenbrier Gardens. We need to answer it. Something could be wrong at the community I haven't gotten any messages there must be something wrong." Alices heart started to race although she managed to stay calm on the outside. Her mind immediately went to her residence wondering what could possibly be wrong, is there a system problem

Thomas asked, "Who's at the door?" in a shaky elevated shout.

"It's me, it's Sean, miss Alice, it's Sean. There's something you need to know. I came as quickly as I could, it's not Greenbrier though everything is OK there"

Alice was relieved to hear that, she calmed down, her heart started to slow a little bit. Thomas began decoding the door locks to allow Sean entrance at Alice's nod

"It's OK, we can have him come in he's trustworthy." "What s sight you are, Sean," Alice said, "Do come in and sit down while you are shaking uncontrollably. What is wrong? Why could you not just telephone me? Why did you need to come all the way here, Sean," she asked

Thomas was immediately taking Sean's vitals then checking everything out on Sean as he sat there talking to Alice. Alice brought Sean to the library next and they all sat down there. "It's all right, Thomas, please let Addie and Beth know I'll be joining you in the kitchen momentarily."

Thomas then glanced at Sean and then over at his mother-in-law, "I think I will stay," he added. "I'll just text talk Addie now with our secret code this young man looks like he seen a ghost and he's in shock I think I need to help him I need to assess him immediately."

Sean was still speaking, he was finding it hard to get the words out, "It's al right, Sean," Alice offered, "You are in a safe place now. Just take it easy. Take a deep breath it's OK I know it's not a Greenbrier emergency you can take your time with whatever it is you need to tell me."

Thomas was placing a large blanket around Sean covering him entirely while gently lifting his right hand to run basic life vital tests. Sean stops shaking so much as soon as he felt the blanket around him and drew a deep breath before sputtering out, "It's uncle Neuman, it's Uncle Neuman he's gone.

"He's gone?" Alice asked in a puzzled voice "I don't understand." Alice looked into Sean's eyes in fear, met hers back.

"Yes, he's gone he's gone," he's time traveled back to 1971.

Chapter 34: Thunder

Crack clap crack clap clap thump. "That's a loudest thunder I think I've ever heard!" Max exclaimed as he looked up. It had grown black in the short time they were talking to Neuman. The storm had just seemed to sneak up on them. People all around were rushing toward the exits in a mad dash to get to their cars before it started to pour down upon them. The rides and attractions were starting to close now. Max turned to Will. "We had better hurry too I'm not sure how our travel will be impacted by the storm chasing us I'm not sure how well it will work." As soon as Max turned to speak, he glanced to the right and left of Will, "Where's Neuman, what happened to him?"

"He was right here right beside me," Will offered, "In the blink of an eye while we were looking at the storm he just disappeared." Will looked at the exit gate just in time to see Neuman, "Look, Dad there he is, he's leaving, let's go, we do not have much time to waste."

Neuman recognized his parents walking toward the exit and in a split second decided to follow them. He just wanted to observe them. While they were young. Alive and well. "Look we're going to get soaked," Neuman's father said.

"Yes, we surely are, Mary," Stevie laughingly responded.

Let's sprint, we can make it to the car," Mary said.

Neuman in his fifty-five-year-old body was doing his very best to keep up with his parents. His mom was seventeen and his dad was eighteen. I just want to see them he said to himself then I will go and meet up with Maxim and Will. Neuman was thinking all the while, huffing and puffing across the gravel and mud filled parking lot.

"Just let's not lose sight of him, son," Max said.

"Well Neuman's no match for me, let me search ahead and catch up to him," and Will took off running while Max followed some steps behind while keeping an eye ahead of the unfolding circumstance.

Mary and Stevie had made it to Stevie's green Pinto car. Neuman stopped and stood just feet away as he watched his eighteen-year-old dad open the passenger door for his seventeen-year-old mom.

"Well, that was fun," Mary exclaimed as she looked back to where the hedges come from.

Neuman's eyes met his mom's and time stood still for both. Neuman saw recognition and love in her return stare into his eyes like they knew each other. Suddenly it started to pour down. "Come on, Mary, we're going to get wet for sure now," Stevie shouted.

Mary Eased herself into the car seat. Stevie closed the car door and went around and got into the driver's seat in a matter of moments they had driven out of sight and out of his life too. Just like when I was nine. They drove off and I waved goodbye and that was it. I never saw them again Neuman said out loud to himself.

"Max and Will were standing by Neuman now the three stood there in solidarity for Neuman. Neuman's tears were streaming down Neuman's cheeks. His tears were undiscernible as the rain was coming down so hard now and drenching them all

Chapter 35: The Walk Back

The walk back to their travel time or their travel zone was hurried and silent. The sidewalks stretched ahead of them with plenty of steps to walk back through the time vortex back to 2042. Max and Will were pleased that they had done what they had set out to do, at least partly. The unplanned surprise of having to help Neuman took up considerable extra time and resources for them, they couldn't finish their mission. Max and Will would now need to plan another trip to the remainder two times to complete the MRP retrieval for Doctor Abrainium. Max could certainly not find fault with Neuman and felt quite relieved that he cooperated much more easily than he had anticipated. Max's experience with Neuman was that of a different disposition. This could have been a real disaster Max thought much worse than this ended up being. The three men stood there at the end of the sidewalk Mac said,

"All set?"

"Will said yes, all set Neuman all set Neuman let me check your time meter let's make sure is completely synced with ours. Neuman reluctantly gave it to Max because it's set for 1974! Max began the process of re calibrating and reprogramming it to 2042 Max handed it back to Neuman after several minutes of re calibrating it. "OK I'm placing this behind you right ear. You don't change this again Neuman."

"OK. We're ready. Let's link arms now and start walking. Think. Concentrate. Focus. Walking down the sidewalk Max linked his left arm with Neuman's right while Will linked his left with Neuman's right arm. The three men started walking together down the sidewalk a few steps before disappearing entirely from 1971 and out of Neuman's family's life. They were walking back into 2042 and back to their lives.

Chapter 36: Sean's Dilemma

"Sean. Alice pleaded. "Please tell me what you mean by that? How could Neuman possibly travel back? What are you talking about? The time travel theory was tested only this week. Max has kept this a complete secret. He discovered and uncovered more information from Doctor A. I don't understand how Neuman would get a hold of this information. Do you know if he spied or gathered information from Max's lab while he was not here? Sean, please help me understand. What answers do you have? I'm now desperately worried about Max and Will's safe return." Alice's thoughts were flooded with Doctor Abrainium's comments earlier in the day about 1971 and Neuman.

Sean looked straight into Alice's eyes. Gazing deeply, Alice felt that he was sincere. "In earnest?" Max questioned.

"Yes," Alice said. "They traveled there earlier today. This was their first time-travel trip after performing many successful tests under all sorts of conditions. They travelled back to help Doctor Abrainium retrieve his memories, specifically around the time when Dr. A. developed his time travel theory. Max and Will's mission is to capture Doctor A.'s memories in 1971, 1974 and 1976. This is the times when Dr. A. was working on his theories and developed them. It is also during this time, that he met and fell in love with his wife, Emily. Using Max's MRP system to capture these memories without disturbing the time that they are visiting, is one of the most delicate issues that they had to deal with and flawlessly prepare for, on this trip. Any disturbance or interruption of anyone's conversation or actions during this trip and memory retrieval, could change the future, our current lives and the time we are living in now. Upon their return, Thomas, with the assistance of Max, Beth and Will are to perform the surgery to insert the MRP chip, with Dr. A.'s memories, into Doctor A.'s hippocampus. The goal and hopeful outcome with this procedure is to assist in the retrieval of Dr. A.'s memory and to remap his memories to lay a new healthy foundation for his new memories to build upon."

Alice was impressed with herself and her intimate knowledge of her husband's work and theories. She needed to say it out loud. This helped her confidence that they would return, soon and their mission would be accomplished. No time interruptions. Sean was surprised with the detail and specificity of Alice's comments. He followed each word. It made sense to him that Max would attempt to do this. Max developed his MRP after all to use only for good and to help others with those who had cognitive disabilities like Alzheimer's disease.

"I'm absolutely beyond upset," Alice said.

"I am equally upset," Sean said. "I am afraid that this whole episode is entirely my fault Alice." Sean attempted a sincere explanation. "I never thought that my uncle Neuman would ever, ever, really be able to time travel. I didn't think that he would be able to do this." Sean repeated himself. Sean continued speaking his thoughts out loud. "This was one of the reasons he chose to travel back to the 1970s. It was because I gave him the information, he needed to complete what he had already determined. Obviously, this last piece of important information about Doctor Abrainium's professional career and history of his life are widely known. However, at Greenbrier Gardens, we have more proprietary information, confidential details of his life. Intimate information like exact dates, times, events, people."

"Yes. Exactly, Sean," Alice replied. "This information is used to help our residents to develop their home environment. We specifically use it to help deliver an individual program and program their personal robot to help them, Sean. We are not to share or use this information for any other purpose. We sign a confidentiality agreement with the resident family members, Sean. You know this." Alice emphasized the word 'know'. Sean rambled on, "I don't know what I was thinking. I breached my agreement with you to maintain complete confidentiality by taking this resident's confidential information. I downloaded Doctor A.'s 1970s history, then I copied it and gave it to my Uncle Neuman earlier this weekend. He seemed so desperately sad, and I was thinking only of helping him. I was not considering the risks and consequences of what sharing this information would result in. I wasn't thinking. I just wanted to help my uncle. You know what it's like with family? You are aware that Neuman has been working on his own time travel theory? I thought this would help him finish it. He was so very close. I was just trying to make him feel better. I did not consider the consequences of my actions as seriously impacting anything with our residents. He said he was going to use the information for good. I believed in him and his pure intent to use the information. But to travel back to 1971? I believe that he wanted to see his parents again. He also wanted to gather some scientific data from the science exhibit at the western fair in return to complete other projects he is working on. It all seemed so harmless," Sean offered.

"Oh, dear Sean!" tears welled up in Alice's eyes. By this time her entire family was looking on from the doorway. "Sean your uncle may have caused irreparable damage to the future. To all of us sitting here now. It's highly likely he has caused damage to our present lives by disrupting the past. I have no words. This makes me feel very ill." Alice offered. Alice shook her head and took a deep breath before turning around to see her entire family standing at the door. They all had concerned looks on their faces. Addie rushed over to give her mum a loving embrace. Alice was sure they had overheard most, if not all, of the conversation. Noting that Jack and Jane Lily's faces were not among them, had Alice quite relieved. She would not have wanted either of them to be privy to this conversation. It would have been difficult to explain. They would be fearful too. "I am glad to see that the children went back to bed."

Addie stepped back from embracing her mum, anxiously asking, "What's going on, Mum? What's happening with Sean? We only caught what I believe is the last part of your conversation. Are Dad and Will going to be all right? What is this all about with Neuman? Are they going to be able to return to us?" Her voice was elevated, and she became shakier with each question, tears welling up in her eyes.

Alice resolutely took control of the conversation. "We can only hope and pray that they find their way safely back. Your dad and Will know what they are doing, are extremely prepared for such possibilities and have trained diligently as such."

Beth was visibly angry. That's how she was dealing with the situation. She was completely devastated to think that her beloved Will may never return. Emotions got the better of her as she strode defiantly up to where Sean was sitting, she yelled at him, "If they somehow don't return, we have you to blame for this, don't we? Don't we? What do you have to say for yourself? Again, I heard you say that you gave Neuman proprietary information! This is reckless! No concern for the dire consequences as a result? All the lives that may be destroyed now or at the least completely altered as a result of your actions! Just what were you thinking?"

Sean stood up and gently took Beth's hands in his, thinking this would help her understand his complete sincere apology. Beth firmly withdrew her hands from his. Sean continued to state, "Please believe me, Beth. I'm so very sorry. I just wasn't thinking about the consequences of my actions. I was in the moment, trying to help my uncle. I was so afraid for his safety. I didn't believe that the information I gave him could be used for him to time travel, or I would never have given him the information." Sean's voice was squeaky and shaky.

Beth stepped further away from Sean. She blurted out "I get that you are sorry, but sorry doesn't cut it! Saying sorry for something that you knew you should not have done in the first place is completely unacceptable! You can't go back and fix this Sean I truly hope for everyone's sake that they return safely and soon."

"Beth," It was Thomas' voice behind her. He gently took her by the elbow and guided her away from Sean. "Let's sit down in the living room for a moment. I have treated Sean for shock he needs to rest now and so do you." Thomas continued to guide his future sister-in-law to a comfortable chair in a corner of the living room. "Why don't we all go into the living room and light a fire? With this thunderstorm raging outside it seems a really good idea. None of us can sleep any way, I'm sure. Sean can continue to rest in the other room. We might as well all be together."

The wind howled through the maple trees outside and made the windows shake. The storm was picking up speed.

Thunder cracked and clapped loudly. Rain suddenly started to pour down in heavy sheets. Beth said, "Setting a fire is not going to help me feel any better. I don't even know if I can sit still."

"Doctor's orders, Beth." Thomas gently but firmly offered before continuing, "We all need to take a breath."

"Beth, you're usually the calm one here. The one who keeps the rest of us on track." Addie said as she gave Beth a big hug. "Let's just sit here a moment, in this room. So many memories for all of us here. Remember Dad and Will are very creative? They left with all of what they needed to get to 1971 and back. They took extra precautions, allowed extra time, and took an extra device to make sure that they would safely return to us. They do know what they're doing." Addie finished.

"I expect them to show back up here any minute." Alice chimed in. Alice was always so optimistic. She was also very confident in her husband's ability and skills. She had great faith that they would find their way back home safely and soon. Alice directed her thoughts to analysing the situation. She shared her thoughts out loud." It's a very good sign that we were all here awaiting their return. If something happened in the past time, then perhaps something would be different among us. We're all still here." Alice looked up and smiled at Beth.

Beth recognized that she made a good point and took a deep breath. "You are entirely right Alice." she said.

Thomas had lit the fire and now it was roaring, creating a warm cozy and calm ambiance to the room. It was a nice contrast to the sound of the constant rain on the roof and the wind at the windows. The thunder was a distant sound now and the wind had subsided a bit. All was calm and quiet in the cozy family den. Sean had settled into the big leather easy chair in the corner of the library, where he was falling asleep with the big blanket still around him. Alice had placed a brown plaid fleece blanket over him earlier. Thomas said "Sean really needs his rest. Sean shared that when he realized what he had done, and that Neuman was gone. He had left a note for Sean. Then Sean raced over here and in this weather. He became distraught, incoherent and afraid. Knowing that telling us this news was the right thing to do, confronting us was the best thing he could do at this point. He was in a state of shock when he arrived here. I am afraid he won't be able to forgive himself."

Quietly Beth, Addie and Alice gazed into the fire. Thomas took a seat beside his wife and gave her a big hug. The McTibbitt's family den. The lamp in the corner gave a soft warm light. The lamp that Alice's grandmother had given her and Max as a wedding gift. The flickering fire casting a shadow on the subdued creamy coloured walls. Walls that held memories of family photos of past generations. The significant events suspended in time sat in frames across the walls and sat in various positions on tables and shelves. Alice and Max's wedding day photo was displayed in a simple silver frame. Adelaide and Will Henry's baby pictures. Their graduations. Addie's prom night. Max's grandparents honeymoon photo on the top of

Whistler Mountain in June. Alice's parents wedding photo capturing the perfect moment that they cut their five-tiered cake. The large, framed photo of last year's Christmas celebration, which captured the entire family enjoying turkey around the family table. Alice was happy to have this moment to look around and to take it all in quietly. As she drew a deep breath, Alice's thoughts drifted to a recent writing in her diary "We are always living in the future traveling through the present bringing the past along with us." "Our home here is filled to the brim with wonderful memories. We are making more right now" she said out loud and speaking to her family in the room. "Let's make them happy and meaningful."

Just then she turned her ear toward the kitchen. A door rattling caught her attention as she strained to determine where exactly the noise was coming from. It wasn't the thunder. "Did the wind get a hold of the kitchen door handle?" she wondered. It sounded like someone was attempting to open the door from the outside. Someone was attempting to shake the door open.

Alice surveyed the room to find that everyone else had also heard the noises. They all looked at each other with questioning looks. "It sounds like it's in the kitchen. Let me go check it out." Thomas offered. He rose from his chair and quickly, yet cautiously, walked toward the kitchen.

"Another midnight visitor? Who could it possibly be this time of night? The security system did not alert us either." Addie asked with concern. "With all our new technology for safety I can't believe this is happening for the second time in one night."

Thomas was at the kitchen door. Beth, Addie, and Alice followed directly behind Thomas. Peeking around the kitchen entrance, curiosity had gotten the better of them. "Who is at the door? Announce yourself please!" Thomas said forcefully. "It's me, Will. It is Will, Thomas." "Will! Oh Will!" Beth squealed loudly and rushed the door.

"Will! "Addie and Alice cried out in unison as they too rushed for the kitchen door. Thomas quickly entered the door code and placed his handprint on the panel. He opened the door to see Will standing there, his larger-than-life presence filling the entrance door frame.

Chapter 37: Back at Greenbrier Gardens

Doctor Abrainium turned the bed knob clockwise revealing the small wooden box, he sat on the edge of his bed opening the lid he took out the yellow folded piece of paper remove the clip he gently unfolded the worn piece of paper. Inside he read the words Remember Me the one who loves you so. More than words. More than time it is time that pulled us apart tonight. And time that mended our hearts. Meet me in your dreams tonight. For hard time. All my love all the time Emily. Doctor Abrainium talked to himself, all my darling Emily I am losing you I cannot remember things like I used to, and I don't want to forget you. For the first time since Emily's passing Doctor A was unable to meet her this evening. He sat on the edge of his bed clinging to the note. The first note that Emily had written to him. He knew that he couldn't remember the necessary pieces to travel back to meet her he was so frustrated. Back to 1970, 1972 to see her, the young woman he loved. Laughing. Telling stories. Asking him questions. She was his life. She didn't know that the entire reason he worked tirelessly on this time travel theory was so that he would never lose her that he would always be with her, and now he was losing her anyhow he was struggling to place his thoughts in order. In a moment of clarity, Doctor A. knew what the future held for him. He desperately wanted to hang on to the memories he had right now. Doctor A. sat on the edge of their beautiful handcrafted solid mahogany bed clutching the little wooden box to his heart. Tears escaped his eyes to run down his cheeks, "I am so sorry Emily," he whispered

Chapter 38

Beth was ecstatic to see well her Will standing in the door. She reached for his hands and gave him a big hug. We were also very worried about you and your dad. I'm so happy you're back!

"Where's dad, Will? I don't see him," Alice exclaimed, "What has happened to him?" she was frantic.

Will put his right arm around his mom and gave her a warm embrace, "I'm not sure, I'm so sorry I just don't know, somehow Neuman was there in 1971 he certainly put a monkey wrench into our plans. We all left together arms linked our time devices were synced. As we walked through the time continuum Dad and Neuman became blurry, they separated and completely disappeared from my sight. Dad and I practiced and tested this over and over these theories these different scenarios. Losing sight of one of us during this time during our walk back we practiced this. Dad told me that if we lost sight of one another not to stop but continue to keep walking through the time continuum. He said the most likely explanation was to get caught in a time vortex or bubble. This may mean that to get back to our time he will have to get through that vortex somehow re-calibrate his time to his device I am sure that if anyone can work through this it's Max that will.," Will said. "I just hope that Neuman didn't do something quite dumb again and cause a problem or delay their return. Neuman had completely different motives to his time travel back to 1971 I can tell you that I believe he wanted to stay there. He even tried to sync his time device to 1974 but dad caught onto it and was able to re calibrate it. This energy could have created the pole in the time vortex for them because of this energy fight. They may be stuck there I believe temporarily, though in time,"

Oh my goodness, Alice responded, "well is there any way we can we do anything on this hand, can we go back to retrieve them can I go back I just want to go back and get him. Oh, isn't there a way to bring them back safely from this time. Did your father give you any instructions on that to bring them back if something happened," she questioned, "He always had alternate theories and processes ready to go if one didn't quite work out."

Alice searched her son's eyes for the answers before he replied. "What can we do, can we pull them back somehow, she asked.

Addie and Thomas were processing Will's words. "I remember that at least on two occasions when I was visiting Dr Abrainium's apartment, I was sure that I heard a woman's voice. I remember wondering if it was his wife Emily's voice that I was hearing and if I was hearing things. Was it possible that he had a way to bring her back though time this way? However, upon surveying his apartment and where I heard the voice come from, I found no one.

Dr. Abrainium was quite alone. He also denied having anyone there visiting with him when I queried him on the voice I heard. Does Dr. A. know how to bring people back through time to the present from the past?"

"That is what dad refers to as a time spirit. A spirit of the person from the past that can travel in time to get through the vortex in the bubble for a short time only. It apparently vanishes quickly though as it is quite fragile. He likened this time spirit to a soap bubble. It breaks and disappears easily and without warning. The encounters are brief. If this theory bears out, then perhaps that is the explanation for the voice that you heard and just as quickly vanished. That won't work quite, Mom, here Doctor Neumann is from this time and traveling back here we cannot travel to the future only to the past and back to our present."

"Yes, I do understand. Your father had explained this to me many times. I have assisted him and watched him and practiced through all these years practiced the theory and tested. But Doctor A. gave me some hope. I didn't have an explanation for what I found with him until now. I know it's possible to move through time as Doctor A. has done it seamlessly on countless occasions it seems. Do you think Doctor A. holds the key to bringing people back to their current time?" he asked.

Thomas said, "Well, we need to come up with a plan immediately to help get Max and Neuman back here to us to our time period yes the answer might be in Dad's lab let's go there and see if there's anything at all, any instructions he left for us in an event like this at this time."

They were all talking over each other explaining what happened, what their theories were, what they could do to help. "You were right it's in his lab," Will said. "I'm trying to get a word in edge weight wise." Will said, "You need to follow me to the lab I'm telling you the answer is there.

"I am glad to see that Paisley certainly stands the test of time, Will," Beth laughed not looking at his shirt.

Alice was already ahead of her family opening her husband's laboratory doors, only she had the code to enter. "What was it, Will, where do we look; I'm surprised that he never told me about this."

"Dad only told me on our way back it didn't occur to him before then he felt that the trip would be flawless and uneventful. It's the artificial intelligence hologram, Mom," Will was talking to his mom and family as he was setting up the AI hologram device. "We must simulate the return Addie, Thomas and Beth made sure to stand back to allow Will the space to do what he needed to do to set this up.

"How can we help, Will?" both asked feeling helpless.

"Nothing to help with," he said. "I am going to set this hologram up of my mom," Will was adjusting the device while the rest of his family looked on

"Well, what on earth do you plan on doing with a hologram of Mum? Addy asked.

"And the time device?" Thomas queried not understanding how it all fit together.

"Well, I'm going to send this hologram of Mom back through time I'm going to set it for 1971 I'm going to calibrate them together then Mum's hologram will come back through time and hopefully disrupt the bubble or the time vortex enough for Dad to continue on his journey with Neuman. Dad had already tested this he believes that it will work. The hologram should interrupt that time vortex and break through it allowing Doctor Neuman to continue on their journey back to us we only have this one chance though."

They all held their breath. "I certainly pray that it works." Alice closed her eyes and sent up a little prayer. "Oh please Lord," she said, "please make it work."

"This is very delicate, let's all be very still, OK, it's all synced, we've got it already." Will hit the time device at the same moment the hologram of his mom appeared propelling it with an old-fashioned fan and then it disappeared

Chapter 39: Caught in Time

"Where are we?" Neuman asked. "I wanted to stay in 1971. When I let go, I thought it would just stay there.

"When you pulled away from Will and you and I were still linking arms, your energy pulled us into a time vortex, Neuman. A time bubble so to speak," Max explained, "You should know this though, Neuman, as you studied this theory too, you should know that now we're suspended in time, we must move through the vortex to get back to 2042 we can't go back."

"How are we going to do that?" Neuman asked, "And what if we just want to go back to 1971," I Neuman.

"It's not possible. Look, Neuman, if you had tested your time travel theory ethically and thoroughly you would have known that this was a possibility when people's energy and focus are pulled in different directions a time vortex can be created. They say time stops for no one, but it looks like we're stuck here in let's see I'm checking 1982 this is 1982 from what I have learned 1982 Oh my gosh no one should be stuck in the 80s and especially not dressed like this, flowered shirt, polyester pants oh my gosh! my parents were still alive," and Max cut him off,

"Neuman, we are not staying here. I am immediately re-calibrating our devices and we are walking right back to 2042 you must promise to stay with me and not to pull stuff like this again. You are putting both of us at tremendous risk as well as events of this time and people in the future. You need to just knock it off! you need a moral compass, Neuman, really. Unfortunately, I haven't developed one yet or I would have given it to you a long time ago. just do us both a big favor here. Do not move."

Neuman had allowed his selfishness to trap him on a one-track mind mission. He had lost control. This had become his life's motivation at all costs. Max understood the importance of family. His own family was the most important thing in his life. However, Neuman's was beyond skewed of what normal was.

Max didn't really know how his life would have turned out without his parents love and support throughout his young and impressionable years. What would life be without Alice by his side he questioned. What about his children Will and Addie, his grandchildren? Still Max thought many people have lived through life changing and traumatic events. Most of them seemed to make smart decisions taking others other people's needs into consideration to make decisions. So, what was it with Neuman? Why was he so different in this? It was 1982 at the western fairgrounds. Max was busy adjusting and calibrating his TTD while Neuman was busy people watching. The song "Jack and Diane" by John Mellencamp was playing over the loudspeakers.

"I just can't get over the hair! Look at all the hair!" Neuman said as he looked around at all the people. Neuman said "It doesn't look like people can see us. Can people see us, Max?"

"No Neuman. People cannot see us. We can see them, but they can't see us because we're stuck in that time vortex that bubble. Now please hand over your TTD so I can re-calibrate it next." Neuman reluctantly handed it over as well as the chip behind his ear. "Well thank you Neuman. This should only take me a few minutes. And then we'll be on our way back to 2042 where we belong."

Max began the process of re-calibrating Neuman's TTD chip.

"A time vortex?" The scary reality started to sink into Neuman's thoughts at that moment. "How are we going to get out of here? We could just die here!" he said. "We may never get out!"

Max tried to ignore Neuman's comments and stay focussed on the task at hand. "Your device seems to have a malfunction Neuman. This is going to take a little bit longer. I need to override it and repair it."

Neuman went quiet. Quiet was his safe default position. He was very worried now. He tried to sit still and stay calm. His left knee would not stop shaking. Finally, after what seemed an eternity to Neuman, Max exclaimed, "OK. problem number one solved. Here's your TTD, Neuman. Let's install this behind your ear now.

"Problem number one?" Neuman asked. "You mean there is more to worry about?" Neuman's voice went squeaky. "Yes. The second issue is, we're still suspended in this time bubble, and we somehow must smash through it to continue our journey." Max said.

"Well can't we use a stone or a pole or something to burst that bubble? There are lots of things I see that we could try." Neuman quipped.

"Not exactly, Neuman. Breaking through the time bubble cannot be done with an object. It doesn't work like that, Neuman. It is within Dr. A.'s theory. There needs to be a different kind of an interruption to break through this bubble. We need a time interruption from another time. I studied Dr. A.'s theory on this and I did prepare for such a circumstance as this."

"I do not recall studying any of this in Dr. A's theory." Neuman added. Neuman abruptly stopped talking, trying to stay calm as he really did remember reading something about this in the confidential material that his nephew, Sean had given him. He had just confessed, and Max would now know he had more information than he had let on. It didn't sound too promising, though.

"Neuman, how would you know about Doctor A.'s theory?" Max narrowed his eyes and frowned at Neuman.

Just then Neuman stood up and pointed straight ahead. "Look! Max! It's Alice! What is she doing here?" Max turned around to see what Neuman was pointing at. People were stopping and staring. They too could see Alice. A young boy exclaimed, "Look! Is that a hologram? Like in the *Star Wars* movies?" "How did a hologram of Alice get here to us?" Neuman was so perplexed he couldn't even finish his next question.

"That my friend, is our time interruption!" Neuman shook his head in disbelief.

"Alice was just here and then Alice had disappeared?"

"Yes. But she was here just long enough to solve our second and last problem, Neuman. Now people can see us. We're no longer stuck in that vortex bubble. Good man Will." Max said under his breath. "Neuman, we have no time to waste."

"Ha Ha! Very funny Max!"

"This time Neuman, we will walk arm in arm and synced. Do not let go! Promise me. Do you understand?" Max was even more serious as he locked into Neuman's arms.

Neuman said. "All right. I promise. Let's go. I am quite hungry now." Max took hold of Neuman's left arm and grasped it as tightly as he could while they both moved forward on their journey back to their own time. Back to 2042.

Chapter 40: Will Returns

Alice took her son's hand in hers. Beth reached for Will's other hand while Addie and Thomas linked hands together with Alice's. All five stood there together as one in silence they felt strong, watching. Waiting. Hoping. "I am confident," Will offered.

"Me too, Add," he offered, "Make that three, no four and five," Thomas said.

Turning to his mom, Will said, "Let's shut things down and lock up here it should be only a matter of minutes now before we know if this worked or not."

"I agree" Thomas said.

Will began the process of putting his dads' devices back in their proper places with everyone's assistance they were done in a good time. Will was the last one to leave and took a good look around before shutting the lab door behind him and entering the code before his mom finished the process to lock it up. The wind started to pick up a bit outside and the rustling of the trees could be heard. Suddenly, the sound of glass shattering on tile floor was heard. The family had just sat down once again in the den. The fire was dying. Sean was sound asleep in the big easy chair in the corner. Then they heard the noise.

Alice jumped to her feet, "What was that?

"Sounded like it came from the kitchen," Will offered. "Let Thomas and I go check it out."

"I'm coming too," Alice said.

They had all sprung to their feet and were hastily almost jogging toward the kitchen.

"Well, that was unexpected," Neuman quipped as he looked around at his surroundings dazed."

"Yes, quite," Max said extending his hand, "Here let me help you up to your feet Neuman."

As Neuman was finding his footing, Will, Thomas, Alice, Addie, and Beth came barrelling in.

"Max, oh Max." Alice's eyes welled up with tears.

"Dad we were thinking, we were ever so worried we weren't sure."

"You are a sight for sore eyes for sure, Max," Thomas gave Max a firm handshake and a welcome back to 2042 Alice gave Max a hug like no other and didn't let go. Even while the other family members tried to hug and greet him.

"I'm so very happy to be home to be here with my family," Max smiled.

Neuman stood in the background looking on. Alice greeted Neuman first, "Neuman, welcome back home to you also."

"Yes, welcome home," everyone greeted Neuman. We are tired and a little hungry. Alice rose to get some of the saved sandwiches out of the fridge while Thomas and Beth gathered dishes and chips with drinks and cookies. It was an instinct for them to pull together and focus on another human need, food and drink a good distraction for us until we are all ready to talk about this. Digest and process all that transpired at the Mc Tibbitts' home in the past twenty-four hours or so. Thomas was taking vitals of Neuman and Max. As the family doctor, Thomas felt sure that they would all get through this together.

Appearing in the kitchen doorway, Sean peered in to see the family bustling around, before his eyes settled on his uncle seated across from Max at the table. His first instinct was to run and give him a big hug. But then he restrained himself as the earth as his anger and fear surfaced as well as fighting with his longing to give his uncle a hug. After a long moment of silence, Sean allowed his relief as he let out a big sigh, "Uncle Neuman, I'm so very relieved that you're finally home safe I was very worried." Sean Stone turned serious as he added, "But you have some explaining to do to me and all of us here, Uncle Neuman.

Chapter 41

The McTibbets' kitchen was a throwback to the last century. Mid-century 50s and 60s to be sure. The stove belonged to Alice's grandmother;s the counters were made of solid wood from Max's parents northern lake home. Cabinets and furniture all scavenged and repurposed from Alice and Max's is family homes. This kitchen and everything in it always makes me feel so good and calm. This is my sanctuary, my safe place to pull back from the world and recharge, Alice thought to herself. I like to do things the old-fashioned way. It helped them stay connected with their family history into themselves as they often work together to prepare meals and entertain family and friends here. Indeed, it was the place of common sanctuary for the entire family. When they entered here, they always stayed. Friends of Max and Alice were impressed that even with all the new technology out today they remained to continue doing things manually. They could have all their meals, snacks and drinks all made for them through voice control automation and have things delivered to them without having to lift a finger. But even serving themselves instead of using their server bots was something that they prefered to do.

"That's certainly hit the spot, Alice, thank you so much," Neuman exclaimed appreciatively.

"You are so welcome, Neuman," she replied.

"That certainly was an exciting adventure the three of you were on today," Thomas added.

"Yes, thank you for explaining what happened," Abbi said.

"Yes, now I want to hear why you did what you did Uncle Neuman," Sean looked right into his uncle's eyes and added rather incredulously yes,

"I am very interested to know too."

Neuman knew he would have to explain to his nephew. Indeed, to a court of law to at some point soon. He had compromised proprietary and confidential information and gotten his nephew into some hot water in doing so. He was tired and wanted to procrastinate, if possible, though. Ownership of the situation was his for the taking. "It's the wee hours of the morning. I would like to wait until after I've had some sleep and start fresh," Neuman responded.

"Well, I will give you that," Sean went on, "but it's not fair what you did. I deserve the full unedited version, honest and detailed.

"Why don't you go up and use the guest bedrooms tonight," Alice graciously offered. "You know that it's not safe to travel in this weather and you cannot leave until we do have your statement and determine next steps," Alice said.

Neuman got up and thanked everyone again and found his way upstairs to one of the McTibbitt's guest bedrooms.

"Now that Neuman and Sean have gone up to bed, I am so very anxious, Max. What happened with the MRP were you able to capture enough of doctor A's history in memory to help him?"

"Yes, Alice, I believe that we have enough of his history in memory to download into his hippocampus.

"And again explain to me, Max, exactly how that process works with the human brain.

Thomas wanted to know, "Yes, Dad, please."

"Well, of course we know that Alzheimer's disease is a long journey disease that commonly affects recent memories, cognitive abilities and judgment. The medication to eventually block the development of the disease needs to begin before the disease process begins in the case of Doctor Abrainium, as well as the other sixteen Alzheimer's disease victims at Greenbrier Gardens, the disease process is already not only begun but, in most cases, progressed to a devastating level. This makes it impossible for the medications to work. It makes it impossible for my MRP to work the way it is supposed to. As you all know I had begun working on this reprogramming theory for many years before the trials were successful and I got the patent and the FDA approval to use. Capturing the affected person's memories before the disease process begins is key to this cure taking one of my tiny MRP chips and placing it in the person's brain before the disease process begins to destroy the person's brain is the best course of action and the best therapy for the cure. In this way the MRP can rewrite the brain's memories on a synthetic map and assure that memories that come in after that will travel along this synthetic pathway well the other part of the present memories now have a map or highway to travel free from tangles rearranged in sequence in an order for doctor Abrainium to regain much of his memory. The older memories form a healthy foundation for which they newer, recent memories can form. It's really a synthetic duplication of what was. Tricks the brain into a present reality really."

"That is extremely fascinating," Thomas exclaimed. "I am just so impressed, Max. We are all just so proud of you, Dad," he said, "being able to work with artificial intelligence for all these years to finally complete this process into reality. And now to be able to help so many people with this technology that have Alzheimer's disease."

"Yes, well, after some much-needed sleep, I'll be able to perform this minor procedure of inserting this tiny chip into Doctor Abrainium's brain. His sons have already signed the consent and waiver for the procedure. Dr. Abrainium understands this and has agreed to the procedure."

"Well, I can hardly wait, if this works as well as you think it will be incredible to speak to Doctor Abrainium learn for from him and all his knowledge. I am beyond excited I can hardly wait to see how Doctor Abrainium fairs with this."

Max was indeed intent on helping those people in his wife's care community all seventeen of them too he hoped. It was part of his calling he believed. To use his gifts and abilities for artificial intelligence technology and brain research. Max thought of his mum and how she succumbed to Alzheimer's disease. And at an earlier age than most. She missed her. Her wisdom, her intellect, her creativity. She realized that her cognitive abilities were dismissed, diminishing in her final years. She was still able to impact great words of wisdom to me. Her words had great impact on my research in eventual artificial intelligence process my MRP although not in time to help her. I am not sure why things happen as they do. Even traveling back in time cannot give me the answer that I seek. Let us live for today and find out tomorrow what we missed yesterday, life happens too fast for words slipping through our hands too quickly are we to take it for granted or find out it's worth? Max could still hear his mom's voice as he smiled remembering that day. Yes, ma'am I have found out the worth.

"My memories are timeless and priceless even with time travel possible, Max," Thomas said tapping him on the shoulder, "Where were you? I think we should all go get some much-needed sleep, in a few hours we will go visit Doctor Abrainium and see if this MRP will really work and save and serve him well and help him."

"I agree pops," Will said.

The McTibbitts clan retired for the evening. Each drifting off to dreamland. Each with a different memory of what had transpired that day.

Chapter 42: Morning Breakfast

Breakfast came early for Dr. Abrainium on this Sunday. He had his favourites. Hot oatmeal with bananas and raisins. Add some milk... "With some blueberries and some orange juice too." Emily's voice echoed in his memory. It was the first morning that Dr. A. could not remember his last evening's visit with Emily. Dr. Abrainium did not realize that he had not visited her last evening. The thought just never occurred to him. Something felt different though. Dr. A. felt sad. He was having a hard time putting his thoughts and feelings together.

"Would you like some ore blueberries, Dr. A.?" his robot Ella asked. Dr. A. sat at his kitchen table, surrounded by his familiar things. He looked around, disoriented before settling his gaze on the robot.

"Who are you?"

"I am your robot assistant, Ella, Dr. A."

Dr. A. went quiet and continued eating his oatmeal with his fingers. Ella stood by collecting information, processing, and storing it to be used to assist Dr. A. Ella was working hard to continually adjusting in the environment, while at the same time assessing Dr. A's vitals and abilities. Ella adjusted her responses. "Where is Emily?" Doctor?" asked Ella.

Another quiet moment went by before Dr. A. got up from the table and walked over to the large window overlooking the beautiful, expansive gardens outside. "She wanted to join us for breakfast as usual."

"I am not sure where Emily is right now, Dr. A. I will check for you. There is a hike this morning at 10 o'clock. You enjoy those Dr. A. Let's get ready and head out. We may see Emily there."

Ella left Dr. A. for a moment to respond to a knock at the door. Alice noticed Dr. A. gazing out of his window and approached him.

"Doctor, it is so good to see you this morning! It is such a beautiful day!"

But Dr. A. did not hear Alice's words. He continued to stare out of the window. Searching. Searching for his memories. Alice was excited for the doctor, and she was confident that she had the news to share with him that would be life altering. There was hope for Doctor A. indeed there was hope now for all her other sixteen residents. the successful adoption of her husband's MRP process. Alice knew that Doctor A"s cognitive ability was declining. She saw him struggling with it daily. Disability to create a new brain memory path for his memories to unlock them, organize them. This would restore his memories short term and long term and create a new path which they could follow and journey. This way he could remember his Emily in full. Alice was excited to make this happen for him.

"It looks like you've had a wonderful breakfast, Doctor A."

"Well certainly all my favorite's, oatmeal with blueberries and bananas, peanut butter, toast, juice and tea," the doctor replied. Doctor A continued to look at Alice, he managed to say, "You know I don't want to be here, Alice." His eyes welled up a little.

She knew from her years helping victims with AD what the doctor a really meant when he said this to her. Not so much the physical space that he was in it was more the place and time, the place in his cognitive ability, his confused state that he didn't want to be in. Despite understanding this and knowing that she was here to make things better her heart ached for him. Alice gently placed her left hand on top of the doctor's right, holding his gaze she said, "I know, I know, and I understand. I'm here this morning though, Doctor A, to share some good news with you. I'm here to hopefully make things a little better."

Doctor A's eyes looked back questioningly but hopefully at Alice. Alice continued, "You may recall, Doctor, my husband, Max, his MRP, well we found out that it works. We have tested it successfully and we think it will greatly help you. Isn't that great news? You shouldn't have to struggle so much with recalling your memories and making sense of them recalling your memories of Emily."

"Yes," Doctor A. responded with a smile. Although he wasn't quite comprehending everything that Alice was saying he did trust her. He felt good about it, he felt reassured in her presence.

"We'd like to set up helping you today, Doctor A. Max and a small clinical team, how does that sound to you?"

Clyde smiled back at Alice nodding his head in agreement, "Good," he said.

"Do you have any questions for me Doctor A.?" Alice asked. Alice needed to ask and wait for his response even though she was unsure he was fully comprehending all her words and their meaning. Doctor A. had signed over his power of attorney equally to both of his sons to make decisions for his health and well-being this is something that Alice had all her residents do before entering the program here at Greenbrier Gardens. Each POA had already also consented to all treatment that Greenbrier Gardens' physicians had deemed helpful for each one but would address it of course immediately before anything was done. Alice had already scheduled a meeting with Doctor A.'s two sons in about an hour to discuss this simple procedure and renew their consents for this specific procedure.

Alice got up from her chair, Doctor A. did also. Alice pushed her chair back in place. "I am here to tell you that you do not have to be here anymore Doctor Abrainium."

Doctor A. managed to say, "Thank you for your kind hospitality. thank you to Winston for helping Doctor A. with everything he needs here."

"Again, thank you doctor a for allowing me to come in and talk to you this morning." Alice left Doctor A.'s apartment with Winston the robot

Chapter 43: Preparation

Alice prepared for her meeting with Doctor A.'s two sons, Miles and Jonathan. She was excited in anticipation for what this would mean for Doctor A. and for all her other residents too. Standing at her computer workstation Alice was drawn to the beautiful sunny day that presented itself outside of her office window. "Another rainbow," Alice said out loud, "how beautiful this is, a good sign of things to come." She smiled, her thoughts then drifted to the events of the past thirty-six hours and of Max. Her family at home. Wondering how they were dealing with the Neuman debacle at home. Poor Neuman and Sean she shook her head before focusing back on her task at hand.

The scientific Ethics Committee we're beginning their investigation of Neuman and Sean today. This committee was made up of three people and one robot. One of the three people had the specific expertise in education in the field of science while another of the people had expertise of laws and regulations regarding this. The third person had neither specific expertise in the science discipline nor had they any law or regulatory experience or knowledge the third person was an outstanding citizen of the community and was present to weigh in on the effects of this on their community. The robot was there as an impartial judge. Once the investigation was complete, the facts would be downloaded into the robot. It would then suggest the next steps and action plan for Neuman and Sean. The committee had the ability to make the final determination based on the robot's outcome. It was a simple and fair process which allowed for the facts to be reviewed as well as the human emotional elements and effects upon the circumstance and the situation. It was also a process that generally was completed within hours instead of days weeks or even months as in days of the past.

Max had completed his answers early, he was now enjoying his time with his family in the kitchen. The committee had since left with Neuman and Sean to go to the main office. "Look Grandma, look Grandpa, another rainbow," Jane Lily exclaimed.

"Yes, I see that beautiful rainbow Jane," Max replied smiling at his three-year-old granddaughter.

"That means lots of blessings today," Jack added with a big grin.

"A great day for us to go shopping then I must say." Addie added winking at her husband, Thomas.

"It means it's a message of hope, of course, that rainbow, after big dark skies there comes a rainbow, a sign of hope well."

"I want to hear about the time travel, Grandpa, I want to hear about the 1970s I want to hear all about it. I want to, I wish I would have gone back to the ancient days," Jack protested.

"Well, I'm happy to tell you about it Jack, Max replied "but Nana and grandpa have a big project that they have to finish today first.

"When can you tell me, Grandpa?" Jack pleaded.

Max put his arm around his grandson to reassure him,

"I promise that I will tell you all about it and answer all of your questions as soon as we finish up this special project today, Jack. Even if we must wait till tomorrow morning, is that OK, Jack?"

"OK, Grandpa," Jack said.

"I want to hear too, Grandpa," Jane Lily said.

"Well, of course, all of us will, we're going to share the story and answer all your questions. Grandpa and your dad and Uncle Will and Beth will be helping with that big project today. You, Jane and I will be visiting the Rainbows and Unicorn mall market today." Addie said

Chapter 44: The Drive

Max gave his voice command to his new Mag Rov for Greenbrier Gardens, making sure all were on board and secured. These vehicles are a dream. Built on a magnetic pole system, they drive themselves, they park themselves. They are self-secured and safe. Eco friendly. "You're all too young to remember the old vehicles that we used to have to drive." Max shared. "They had tires instead of gliders, they used gas instead of magnetic force. I had to get a special permit and license to operate one. My! How times have changed the past couple of decades."

"I know that, Dad," Will spoke up. "I've seen those old photographs and images. Pretty wild! How could you possibly be productive when you're traveling somewhere, you had to use manual drive for a vehicle? Blows my mind!" Will continued to ask questions. "Hard to imagine it now even after I have visited the 1970s and 1980s. I see how it all used to work up close."

"I can't imagine a life without a basic sophisticated communication system." Beth chimed in. "I can't comprehend how you communicated to one another without nexting, texting and thoughtexting. I am happy to be alive and well in the year 2042."

"Our past has brought us here though. Taught us many things and given us great insight. Without our past we wouldn't have this present or future for that matter." Thomas added.

"How are you feeling about the MRP chip implementation for Doctor A. today?" Beth asked changing the subject

"I'm excited to be in a good position to help Dr. A." Max responded. "The MRP has been successful with many Alzheimer's victims capturing their memories in real time, within the patients' brain. The unknown element about this procedure is that I was the one that went back in time and captured the memories on Doctor A.'s behalf. I'm not sure how this is going to work as a second person host, but I did capture the memories on the MRP, and we will insert it so I have every hope that this will be completely successful. And I'm confident that we were able to capture enough of Doctor A.'s memories in the 1970s and then in the 1980s. The MRP chip implant procedure is a simple procedure now that I've performed so many safely and successfully. I've seen your work in the results, amazing surgeon Thomas together with my chip design your magic skills best DNA and map guide system and Will's artificial intelligence monitoring system development, virtually no more Alzheimer's disease exists in our modern world. Except for those seventeen people that we cited Greenbrier Gardens well we are all ready for this as ready as we're ever going to be. It will be another first for our team though."

Alice's hologram image appeared and she started to speak while they were traveling, "All systems go here, I have a lengthy conversation with Doctor A., son in showing the procedure and the results. There are 100% on board with this procedure and of course they're hoping for the best, they're actually very excited," Alice said.

I see that you have all arrived the Mag Rov pulled up and hovered to allow all passengers to embark the craft. "Please park," Max commanded the vehicle.

"Yes. Sir," the vehicle responded.

"That Navy navigator package you got Dad is a kick Will laughed as the group entered the front part of the foyer of the building. It was now 12:45 PM. The procedure would be completed by 1600. They noticed how successful it was by 2100 that evening. Alice was there to greet her family with hugs, escorting them down the hall and the immediate corridor to the left. The corridor houses the clinical IT and AI areas of function. This area was closed to residents and guests with the exception of course of the health area and the healthy U area. This area provided private space for residents to visit with their own physicians or for procedure or for their families in all three.

Entering the waiting area sympathetically designed and altered to Doctor A's tastes, the team was greeted by Jonathan and Miles and Doctor A. was there as well. "Good to see you again Miles," he said as he extended his hand to Max with a broad smile. Jonathan also stood up and shook Max's hand next with an odd,

"Let me introduce the rest of my team here," Max said.

"Dr. A. These are the other physicians making up the rest of my team that will be assisting you today." Alice said speaking directly to Doctor A. "Along with my husband, Max, whom you know and the developer of the MRP. Let me introduce Dr. Thomas Cameron, the neurosurgeon. Dr. Will Henry McTibbits a general anesthesiologist and artificial intelligence integration surgeon. And this is Beth Anderson my son's fiancé' and brain genetic mapping clinician." Alice knew that Doctor A. would be a little confused even though she had spent the past hour walking him through the steps of the procedure. This was a lot of information to process. Alice gave Dr. A. the benefit of the doubt though. He certainly would have no problem understanding all of this if it weren't for his cognitive disability. Because of his intellect and background, Alice explained it to him which gave him dignity and respect.

"We are so happy to be with you today to help with you," Alice reassured him taking, his right hand in hers. "We are equally happy that you and your family have agreed to this procedure today. Do you have any questions for any of us, Dr. A.?"

Dr. A. hesitated as he gathered his thoughts to ask the only question that mattered most to him. "Will I still be able to visit Emily afterwards?"

Miles stepped up closer to his dad to answer this for Alice. All the while thinking, "This is why we are all here today. To stop this bizarre behaviour and have our dad back."

Alice, however, had already started to speak. "This procedure will give you the ability to remember Emily fully as well as all your other family members and memories. Past and recent. This is our hope for you, Dr. A. Your ability to visit Emily will be up to you as it always has been."

There was a long silence as Dr. A's two sons looked on, waiting for their dad's response. With his gaze still fixed on Alice's face, he nodded his head and quietly responded, "Ok."

Alice smiled back at him and stretched out her hand for him to take it. "I will be with you all the way. Come with me and I will show you the way." Alice's presence was very reassuring to Dr. A. As she linked her arm with his and led him through the tall, frosted glass doors, into the pre-surgery area, he turned and waved to his sons. Overhead, the song "American Woman" by 'The Guess Who' was playing. Dr. A. remarked. "Why, you are playing one of my favourite songs!"

"Really? Dr. A. I thought you might like some 1970's music today. And apparently now, after their trip back there, Max and Will are really liking it too!" Music. So very powerful, thought Alice.

Once inside the pre-op room, Dr. A. was relieved to see two familiar faces. Nurse companion Jenny was there and gave him a big welcoming hug. Ben stepped up and clasped both hands over Dr. A.'s right.

"Welcome Dr. A.! We are your dedicated assistants today."

Alice felt any anxiousness leave the room when she saw how Dr. A. interacted with Ben and Jenny. She too remained calm on the outside trying not to allow any of her anxiousness to show through on the outside. She attributed any of her anxiousness to her just wanting so badly for this procedure to work out perfectly for him. Of it also impacted outcomes for her other sixteen residents. "You are in good hands here, Dr. A., with Jenny and Ben. I am going to let them take over now and get you ready. I will be back shortly though to escort you into the operating room."

Alice made her way back to the waiting room and Dr. A.'s two sons. "Your dad is very calm and reassured that all will go well. I am completely confident in my husband, Max's, abilities as well as the rest of the team." Alice offered.

"If we did not agree with you, Alice, we would probably not be here today. We are looking forward to having our dad back, as we have said so many times. We must sound like a broken record," Miles responded.

"I will be back to check on you a bit later with updates. We have a variety of snacks and refreshments her for you to enjoy in the meantime." Miles and Johnathon thanked Alice as she left out the door she came in.

Upon peering onto the pre-op room, Alice saw Dr. A. on his gurney, very relaxed and asleep.

She promised to be with him all the way. She would be with him albeit she would be watching the whole procedure on the other side of the OR through a window.

Alice took her seat in the OR observation room. Although Alice was also a Geriatric Physician, this surgery was not within her scope of expertise and there is such a thing as too many Dr's in the OR. Max, Beth, Will and Thomas with the assistance of three surgery bots, four specialized nurses, and three surgical technicians had the room all set up for the procedure. As a team, they had completed this procedure many times. They could not have prepared any more than they had despite the unknown outcome today. There was no way to know until after the procedure.

Alice watched as Jenny and Ben accompanied the surgery bots with Dr. A's gurney into the OR. Each robot had a specific function. One was to guide the entire procedure from start to finish with each surgeon's part. One was there to monitor the patient and vitals, making any necessary adjustments. The third robot's specific task is to administer and monitor the anesthesia.

"The technology of surgery today has certainly progressed", Alice thought to herself. "Not at all like when I went to Med school so many years ago." The entire surgery protocol is on a tiny chip inserted to the back of the surgeon's ears. This provides complete guidance to Max and the entire team. The robots keep the entire process flowing and perform tasks that keep the surgeons focussed on the procedure at hand. "Marvelous." Alice said to herself. "No room for error. Not with all our advancements."

The procedure had begun, and Alice realized that she was watching history being made. Her eyes went to the large screen above. About ninety minutes went by. The tiny MRP chip had been securely installed in Dr. A's brain. Alice took a deep breath. Beth and Thomas's part was second in the procedure as they worked to build the new memory map. Next, Will Henry integrated the A.I. system with the chip before Max came back in to test it. Now the moment of success was upon them. A harmless temporary dye was administered into the chip to show the simulated path. Was it there? Would it work? They all just stopped inside the OR. Waiting. Watching. Everyone was on pins and needles. Breaths held. Looking up at the big screen overhead, they were able to see the purple dye follow along the map's synthetic path that they had all had a part in building. ninety seconds passed before, 'There it is! There it is!" Max excitedly yelled out. They all gave themselves air high fives.

Max looked up to see Alice standing up against the window. She blew him a kiss and then put both her arms up in the air. "Yahoo!" Max and his team turned their attention back to Dr. A to finish the procedure.

This was a fantastic and exciting moment in history! Alice was so excited for Dr. A. His family. Her other residents and their families. "I can't get too ahead of myself though," she thought. "We need to wait and observe Dr. A. for the next seventy-two hours or so. Perhaps even longer to see if there were any complications from the procedure. I will wait until they move Dr. A. to the recovery room before I go to speak to his family."

Alice was bursting with excitement to share the success with them.

Chapter 45

Meanwhile, on the opposite side of Greenbrier Gardens, the staff were hosting a family training and integration day. Greenbrier's program required their resident's families to participate in the training program as well as play an active and regular role in their care five days per week. Today's program was "Walk in My Shoes for A Day". At the start of the day, each family member was given a pair of shoes that fitted perfectly and AI simulated a day of everything their loved one went through on an earlier day that week. Once the shoes were on, the family member experienced the entire day by walking through step by step, everywhere they went, what they said, ate, drank and even what they had been feeling. This was a wonderful way for families to really understand what their loved ones experienced and ultimately help them once they returned home. The families were enjoying themselves and the interaction with their loved ones today. This part of the program had a powerful impact on their understanding of where their loved was in the disease process.

Chapter 46

"Why Neuman!" Addie exclaimed. Addie had just arrived back home from The Rainbows and Unicorns Pavilion with Jack and Jane Lilly. "I certainly didn't expect to see you again so soon."

"Hello Dr. Neuman," Jack said, waving towards Neuman.

Jane Lily just stared at Neuman. Not too sure she should say anything. But then she decided to blurt out, "You are free."

Neuman smiled at Jane. "Yes, they did let me go. Both Sean and me. But not without our list of obligations."

Addie gave Neuman a glance as to say no more of this type of chatter in front of the children. "Neuman, why don't you help me bring in our packages?" Addie asked. "After we get settled in, you could stay for some tea?" she asked Neuman.

Neuman obliged and said, "Yes Addie. I would like that."

Where is Sean today?" Addie asked as they entered the kitchen.

Neuman replied, "Sean began his remediation obligation at Greenbrier today." Neuman was happy to assist Addie although this was part of his obligation part of his remediation. For what he had done. He did hold a soft spot in his heart for Max and his family. When he was with them, he felt a certain sense of belonging and calmness. Something he had been missing for most of his life after losing his parents to that tragic car accident so long ago when he was only nine. His only sibling, his sister Martha, gone now too so many years ago. Neuman's jealousy of Max's family and successes were the ugliest part of himself that he had to that he had to battle with daily.

"Where would you like these placed, Addie?" he asked.

"Oh, you can leave them right there in the hallway, Neuman, thanks so much."

"Can we have some ice cream, Mommy, ice cream," Jane Lily asked.

"Well, you know you can't just eat ice cream, Jane," Jack answered her.

"I know," Jane Lily said.

"First you must eat something healthy," Jack said'

"That's right. I have peanut butter wraps and fresh fruit salad with milk," Addie offered.

"Oh that sounds good and then ice cream, Mommy," Jane Lily squealed.

Addie just laughed. "Please have a seat, Neuman. I have some other protein wraps as well if you don't like peanut butter."

At the kitchen table Neuman took a seat on the side opposite both children. They were noticeably hungry and very quiet as they ate their lunch. Addie handed a beautiful plate of fruit, cheeses and protein wraps with biscuits and joined them at the table.

"This looks splendid," Neuman said. "I thank you for the lunch, Addie I won't be able to stay too long I do have a list of obligations I need to start today. It's already been quite a day for me. Quite a few days. Part of my obligation and remedy is helping you and Max. As well as Thomas, Will Henry and Beth of course Alice as well. I am scheduled to complete the plan review with your family within twenty-four hours and then repeat this first step back."

"Well, Mom and Dad will be back late tonight I believe."

Neuman got up and decided to leave and had headed for the door he turned around and he said, "Well thank you again so much Addie it's good to see you."

"Well, you are quite welcome, Neuman we will see you tomorrow then, I'm sure." Addie smiled at Neuman before closing and reprogramming the door. Addie's attention was all about Jack and Jane noticing their plates were clean. "Well, it looks like it's time for ice cream at she said."

Chapter 47

At 2100, Doctor A was regaining his consciousness now and resting comfortably in the cozy recovery room. Although the procedure took longer than they had planned for, the team was confident that it was a complete success. Jonathan and Miles were anxiously waiting for their dad to regain complete consciousness from this procedure. His robot nurse was standing by as well as Jenny and they both continued to monitor his vitals and responses.

"Dad, how are you feeling?" Miles asked standing by the bedside. Jonathan was standing beside Miles, they were both anxiously hoping for a cognitive clear answer from their dad.

Doctor A's eyes were open, and he took a moment to survey his surroundings before resting his gaze on the two young men standing before him. Then he responded. "I am rather hungry right now, Miles, I should think that your wife Gracie's homemade stew and biscuits would suit me just fine right now."

Jonathan and Miles looked at each other somewhat dumbfounded, however, obviously very happy. Jonathan spoke next. "I'm quite sure we can arrange that, Dad. Right Miles?" he asked.

Both sons could not contain their happiness. They could not stop smiling, grinning ear to ear. Tears welled up in Mile's eyes, despite his happiness. He was also in disbelief. "I'm just so very happy to have you back, Dad."

"Yes, Dad. We are overjoyed!" Jonathan offered while going in to hug his dad. Hugs were an overdue bonding moment for the three of them. Both sons embraced their dad tightly, not wanting to let go.

"I'm happy to be here in this moment, with my two sons," Doctor A. said. "But I don't understand your comment about my absence, Miles, about me not being here. I haven't gone anywhere. I've been right here all along. You stopped seeing me for a while." He paused before continuing, "I understand that I had a procedure and now I'm recovering, but I haven't gone anywhere."

Jonathan looked at Miles with a questioning face as if to say, "Dad has a good point."

Miles responded to his dad, "Dad. We're just so happy that you were doing so great after your procedure. I understand that you will be coming home with us tomorrow after a night of rest here for observation." Jonathan added.

"Yes, they just want to monitor you for the next twenty-four hours. It looks like you're good to go, Dad. They just want to make sure." Miles said.

"Your grandchildren are going to be so excited to have you back home!" Jonathan said.

Clyde grinned as he thought of the fun he was going to have. For the first time in a long time, he felt that his thoughts were his own. He could organize his thoughts. He could control them. He could decide which thought to bring forward or he could introduce other thoughts. There was not something else taking over. His memories were in sharp focus. His mind was clear. He didn't feel anxious or angry. It all felt so normal. Yet, new for some reason. His thoughts started to drift to his past. He found himself delighting in thought about his life with his two sons, his daughters-in-law and his three grandchildren. Birthdays, holiday celebrations and anniversaries presented themselves in detail. The births of each of his grandchildren showed up next. Holly, now fourteen, Hunter, twelve and Cornelius ten. Emily was there in every thought and memory. After all, Emily was there, right beside him, for each of these milestone events. He remembered how excited she was to become a nanna for the first time. And then the second time and the third time too. Clyde remembered this easily and in right sequence. He remembered their first grandchild was more like an extravaganza. Clyde recounted the first shopping experience for granddaughter, Holly with Emily and chuckled to himself. He had told her then, fifteen years ago now, that Emily had the ability to make even the simplest of life's tasks into an adventure of celebration. Clyde closed his eyes in the recovery room. He was enjoying reminiscing about that day, lost in his special daydream. His sons both gave him a kiss on his cheek with a big hug.

They sensed he needed to rest now. Saying goodbye, promising to be back later.

"It's time to go now if we are to make our appointment Clyde!" Emily said. He remembered that rare day when she was on time. She made a playful point of letting him know. Instead of doing a virtual walk-through visit in 'Baby Beginnings' section of the 'Vast Warehouse', Emily insisted that they make an appointment for an in-person experience. "I want to see, touch and smell the items that will be an intimate part of my grandchild's life Clyde."

"I quite understand Emily," Clyde gently replied. "I know you wouldn't have it any other way."

"Emily. The artist, painter, tactile indulgence was a core part of who she was." Clyde thought to himself. That day found them roaming up and down the long aisles in their reserved mag rove cart. Emily considered floating baby beds, sleepy soft quilts, learning toys, baby wrist monitors, baby carts and baby clothing. "Look at this Clyde!" holding up a giraffe inspired gray white and fluffy yellow sleeper. "I cannot remember Miles or Jonathan ever being this little. Do you? Let's get them all! A whole week's worth of changes." Clyde was relieved to hear Emily say a week's worth of changes, which was just seven, or so he thought. Clyde was mindful of their budget, but on this day, he knew their budget would not be a priority.

"Emily. That seems perfectly reasonable." Emily chimed in, "How many changes per day? Is that seven, eight, nine?"

Clyde quickly did the math in his head. "Oh, my dear!" he said under his breath. "I know Jonathan and Martha will be very happy and grateful for Emily's thoughts of reason."

"We will get a week's worth of changes for baby's first year." He remembered hearing Emily say. He also remembered being speechless at that point. Clyde's eyes nearly fell out of his head. "We will need sizes infant, three months, six months, nine months and twelve months."

Clyde laughed out loud. What else could he do? "My goodness Emily," he gently chided. "Do you think that we should leave something on the shelves for the other grandparents and family members to buy?"

"We're purchasing just the essentials and some fun things too. Don't worry! There's going to be plenty of items for other people to buy."

Clyde looked at the list again, grateful that their son and daughter in law's first vacation home was not on the list. Emily laughed at Clyde's words. She was such a giving, generous soul. It was difficult for Emily not to try and take care of everybody and everything. "Clyde, I do think that we have enough for today. We may need to return another time. This is a good start."

"Yes. I agree, Emily," Clyde said as he looked at the many digital note items accumulated in their cart. Clyde remembered that day so well. Holly decided to make her grand entrance into her new world, on that very day. She was two weeks earlier than they had all anticipated or planned for. It was touch and go for a couple of weeks after that before bringing this precious little life home. Jonathan and Martha were so very grateful for Emily's and Clyde's timely purchases. It really helped them. Holly's new digs were complete and ready for her in plenty of time.

"Emily must have known something the rest of us did not." Emily's uncanny intuition told her that having everything in place in time was crucial to making everything easier on the new mom and dad. 'Getting the practical, logistics out of the way in order to enjoy the magic is important.' she used to like to say. And at no other time did this hold true than that on this glorious occasion. The birth of their first grandchild. She arrived so precious and so very tiny.

Emily's eyes were filled with happy tears the first time she held little Holly in her arms. "Look Clyde! She is smiling at me. Hello little Holly. I am your nanna."

Darling little Holly. Clyde remembered. Not so little anymore at fourteen. Holly is strong, smart and happy. Level-headed and not afraid to speak her mind. She's following in her parents' footsteps although she's a lot like her grandmother. How very proud her family is of her. Miles' two sons, Hunter and Cornelius are growing into fine young men too. Smart, kind and respectful. Clyde said to himself. I couldn't be prouder of my whole family. Clyde continued in his dream-like state, his thoughts turned again to Emily. Tears flowed down his cheeks.

Clyde remembered Emily, He remembered that she had been gone now for over seven years. And this time, this fact registered and stayed with him. He remembered visiting her every evening. He needed to visit her again tonight. He had a question for her. Drifting off to sleep he whispered to himself, "Remember Me. the one who loves you. more than words, more than time. It is time that pulled us apart but time that will mend our hearts. Meet me in your dreams tonight, for heart time. All my love, all the time, my sweet Emily. I miss you so."

Chapter 48: Our Memories

It is a sweet yet tortured happiness we all find in our memories. At times we choose to be selective in what we remember. But most often we have no choice, our experiences dictate and unfold, weaving in and out of our lives creating lasting memories stored in our mind. Our memories exist there, locked in storage compartments to be unlocked and retrieved at our beckoning at our will. For those of us unfortunate enough to have stored memories that we cannot retrieve anymore or at our will or a beckoning, yet they are there locked and filed away, our ability to call upon them put them in order to make sense of them all gone with cognitive or memory impairments. Our judgment too, goes along with it. Reality becomes skewed memories come tumbling down, falling out all over the place. A cure for Alzheimer's disease I have always believed that it would not be a medication type therapy. I believe that it will be an artificial intelligence process. A memory chip to recreate the memory route, regardless of the deterioration on a victim's brain. Within the course of everyday conversation, lost our ability to complete simple tasks or to unconsciously retrieve a memory. The ability to zip up a sweater, tie one's shoes or brush our teeth. The need for this assistance is what leads those needing this assistance to be segregated from all others in society. From one's own family. These people were relegated to an undignified ending, to a sweet life of memories forever lost. That was until the memory retrieval process was discovered. This exciting process of retrieving our memories. Remapping them, building the foundational bridge for our newest memories to follow along. Filling in the lapses and voids, to be retrieved later. Memories meant to be shared with others. Memories that make us who we are. Without them we are empty shells. What memories we all have! What stories we have. Doctor A. had this now. His hope and new beginning. All other Greenbrier residents at Greenbrier Gardens now also had this same wonderful opportunity. Max had attributed this success for Dr. A. to his MRP being an absolute miracle. He took many risks and chances. Now it could be successful for the sixteen others that missed the cure. This would be completed soon. Max's time travel formula and process was now securely housed. Neuman and Sean were to carry out their appropriate and closely monitored sentences of doing only good deeds for their community. Their sentences became their choices too. They chose to move forward making only good memories.

Chapter 49: Dr. Abriainium's Secret Validation

Doctor Abrainium did meet Emily in his dreams that night as he did every night since. They danced together. They laughed, delighted in their shared sense of humour. They walked hand in hand and embraced each other tightly. 'All this down memory lane' or so he told his sons. Myles and Jonathan were indeed so very happy to have their dad back with them and making a lot more sense. No more talk about him visiting their deceased mom anymore. It was three months past the procedure and things were going well. "Certainly a miracle, Alice," Jonathan stated.

"Yes, everything is as if he never acquired Alzheimer's Disease."

Alice smiled compassionately at Miles as he added. "We're back to being one cohesive and healthy family now with much thanks to you and Max. We can't thank you enough."

"Your whole family, Alice, has been absolutely wonderful!" Jonathan added. "I don't know nor do I need to understand how that whole MRP map process works. I'm just so glad that it did! And I understand that your other residents are all in the process of at one stage or another of having this therapy too."

"Yes. Max and I are so excited to be in this position to help them." Alice said.

Doctor A. was quietly sitting in a large easy chair beside his two sons. He was deep in his thoughts again. "Doctor A.? Would you like to take a walk with me? I have something to show you that I believe belongs to you." Alice turned to Miles and Jonathan, "If you don't mind? We will be back in a few moments," Alice said.

Doctor A. rose from his chair, "Of course, Alice." Arriving at the door of what was once briefly, Doctor A.'s home at Greenbrier Gardens, Alice waved her hand to open the door. Stepping inside, Doctor A. followed her. "I have found something that I believe belongs to you Doctor A. Something that is very important to you." Alice motioned toward the bed knob. Dr. A. walked over and turned it to the right and then to the left. Doctor A reached in and took out the small mahogany box. Tears came to his eyes as he sat on the side of the bed looking down at the little box.

"I thought that I may lose, this forever. Thank you, Alice." he said.

"Oh, yes of course. I wanted to leave everything as it was until you had a chance to make sure you got everything back that you needed. I understand that your sons are arranging for all your things to be moved to your new home, a cottage on Miles's property tomorrow.

"Yes. that's right, Alice. I am really looking forward to being close to my family and making more memories." Dr. Abrainium offered.

"When the housekeepers were dusting yesterday, they told me that the bed knob fell off and onto the floor. They alerted me about this. When I checked it and attempted to repair it, I noticed that there was a small object inside the hollow bed post. I left it undisturbed. I placed the knob back on and waited to show you. I wanted to make sure that you had it safely back in your possession. I didn't want it to get lost in the move. I had a sense that this was something meaningful to you."

Clyde looked up at Alice and smiled. "Yes. This is especially very dear to me." Clyde stood up placing the little box inside his jacket pocket.

Alice knew that Doctor A. needed this to visit Emily. She had learned this from Max and his recent time travel experience. Alice knew Dr. A's secret. But neither mentioned this as they left the apartment. Instead, they walked down the hallway chatting about horses and the weather until they were back where they started from. His two sons were there waiting for their dad.

"All set then, Doctor A.?"

"Yes. Thank you, Alice. Remember me." Dr. A. said with a wink.